BEYOND TOMORROW

Wayne Fox

The author when leaving the Navy in 1959

Author: Wayne Howard Fox
Comments to: navytailhook1@gmail.com

Printed in the United States of America

First Printing: February 2019
Second Printing: July 2019

Wayne Howard Fox

ISBN-9781798048092

Forward

The story in this book is fiction. I did fly the Navy fighters that are mentioned in this book. I also flew off an aircraft carrier. This has given me the knowledge to write about these planes with detail and accuracy. I served in the US Navy for over seven years in the 50s and acquired 2,000 hours of flight time and over 4,000 landings during those years.

The Korean and Vietnam wars did take place, but the events portrayed here may not be actual events. The French Foreign Legion did fight the Viet Minh in Vietnam, and the battle at Dien Bein Phu did occur with the French losing. The French Foreign Legion used the F8F Bearcat that had been acquired from the US. The characters are fictional. The US later entered the war in Vietnam. It was a very costly war in terms of human lives.

I have tried to portray, in the Korean war, that our forces fought with restrictions imposed on them that not only hindered their progress, but were also costly in human lives. These restrictions were carried over when the US joined the fight in Vietnam with the same results. Both wars were unpopular wars with the people at home.

Some people at home blamed the US fighting man for the carnage that took place in Vietnam. Some voiced that opinion openly, even to the extent of very likely causing the death of some of our military personnel imprisoned in

Vietnam. I feel it should be noted that these men did not want to be in Vietnam and certainly did not want to risk their lives fighting but had to by order of the US President. Later that attitude did change with the American people, and the true reason of why they were there was acknowledged.

There are atrocities committed when people are engaged in killing each other. It's not right for these to occur and often difficult to understand.

This book is dedicated to the men and women who had to fight, and some even die. I think the American people now realize just what they did, why they did it, and who they did it for. It is very common now to have someone thank me for my service. I accept it for the honor of those who died and all who served.

Wayne Fox

CHAPTER I

I felt a hand on my shoulder and a voice that said. "Max! Wake up you're scheduled for a 0500 launch. Be in the ready room in fifteen minutes. You'll be launching in the dark, so put on your red goggles."

"What's up?"

"Got some Marines who are having a rough time near Chosin. They need some help, so we'll get planes in the air as soon as possible. The fighting died down a little during the night, but they expect to be hit hard around daybreak. There will be coffee and sandwiches in the ready room."

"I'm on my way," I replied as I put on my flight suit, grabbed my .38 revolver, and slipped on my red goggles. The rest of my gear would be in the ready room or at the airplane. I took the time to step out on the gun tub that was just outside our bunk room. We were getting some light rain with a low ceiling. The sea was rolling, driven by a twenty-five to thirty knot wind, which had its effects on the ship. The launch would not be too bad, but the landing would be interesting with a five or more degree roll of the deck accompanied by some pitching as well. Those Marines have it a lot tougher than that, I thought to myself, so I'm sure not going to complain.

As I walked into the ready room, I put on my life jacket and helmet while checking to see that my oxygen mask was properly attached. I got some coffee and a sandwich and took my seat. The briefing started right away.

Our skipper, Commander Welsh, went to the front of the room hesitating for a moment. "Gentlemen, we have some of our comrades in trouble. They need our help. We, with God's help, will give them that help. The casualties have been high. They have not been able to get reinforcements to them, so it is up to us to stop the enemy from overrunning them.

We'll go in with four planes followed by four more and so on. Each flight will return to the ship, rearm, and go back. That way we can keep a near constant attack going. We don't want them to have any time to reorganize. We want them confused and ducking. That way, they can't do a good job of fighting our Marines. Our sister carrier, Wasp, will coordinate the attack with us. Combined we will have about one hundred fifty planes available for the attack. We should be able to level the area around the Marines to give them a way out. We think the enemy is at battalion strength which far outnumbers the Marines."

The Skipper hesitated. "Be sure of your target. I don't want to hit our own men. If you have any doubt, don't drop or shoot. The Marines will try to define their lines. This will probably be with smoke grenades. At times, the two lines may be almost on top of one another. They will be very difficult to recognize. Again, if you are not sure, don't fire. Any questions?"

One of the flight leaders stood up. "What about downed pilots, can we expect someone to pick us up?"

"That is affirmative we will have choppers in the area that will try to pick you up, but that may not be possible with all the enemy around. If you have a buddy down, try to stay with him as long as possible. Be sure to put out a location on him. If you have damage, but can stay in the air, try to make it to the water before you eject or ditch. We will try to keep track of safe areas on land if we can. Any questions?"

None followed. "You have the schedule, let's go help our Marines."

I was in the first flight, so I scrambled for the flight deck and our planes. We were members of VF-21, flying the F9F-5 Panther jet off the Philippine Sea. Lieutenant Don Worth was our flight leader with Ensign Dale Rogers as his wingman. I, Lieutenant junior grade Max Bradley, was the section leader in the number three spot. My wingman was Ensign Jake Wells. Don and Dale's planes were already on the catapult with mine and Jake's right behind them.

We were in our planes in seconds waiting for our plane Captain to give us a thumbs up to start our engines. The Auxiliary Power Unit was plugged in and running. We wasted no time in starting our engines and doing a quick pre-takeoff check. Our plane Captains had done the pre-flight check before we arrived. The carrier had already turned into the wind, picking up speed for our launch. The launch officer was standing between Don and Dale's planes. He gave Don the signal to go to full power. He stood facing Don waiting for the salute from Don saying he was ready. When Don saluted, the launch officer dropped his arm and pointed down the deck telling the catapult operator to activate the catapult. Don's plane was hurled into the air, accelerating at over a hundred mile per hour in two hundred feet. The launch officer had already turned to Dale with the same procedure being reacted again. I was almost in place on the catapult before Dale had cleared the deck. Jake and I both went through the same procedure. We had four airplanes in the air in less than four minutes.

We quickly joined up in formation before we entered the clouds and headed for North Korea. We broke out in the clear at about ten thousand feet, finding a warm greeting from the sun. As we climbed higher, the sun became more visible. It seemed to be welcoming us to a new day, a day that could hold many surprises.

I offered a prayer asking to be forgiven for the men I knew I would have to kill. I also asked for our safety and safe return to our ship. The safety of our Marines on the ground was last.

We leveled off at thirty thousand feet while continuing inland. It would take less than an hour to arrive over our target. I tried to relax but found that almost impossible. Don came up on the radio to contact the forward air controller for instructions and update on the situation. He received an almost immediate response asking for our estimated time over the target, what we were flying, and the ordinance we were carrying. The conversation then turned to the current situation with the Marines.

It went like this. "It has been a rough night trying to hold our position. Mortar shells have been coming in all night. We are dug in, but we have had more casualties. We are completely surrounded with no way out. The enemy is at battalion strength, so we have no chance of fighting our way out. We are low on ammunition; we need more now.

We've been promised a drop as soon as it is light enough to do so. They did try a drop during the night, but we only received part of it. We need your help. How far out are you?"

"We will be there in less than 10 minutes. Can you give me an estimate of your ceiling and weather?"

The controller promptly returned with, "I would estimate our ceiling at between three thousand and four thousand feet. We have some light rain."

Don replied. "We just entered the clouds at ten thousand feet and should break out soon. I think we are just south of your position. Try to mark your perimeter with smoke grenades. Give me a yell as soon as you see us. We may need directions in case we don't see you right away. Our first run will be with our cannons, so we can see where to put our bombs, but that is flexible."

After a short pause, "I can hear you now, I think you may be southeast of our position. I have ordered some smoke be put out for you."

Don came back with. "We are out of the clouds, and have a visual on you. We are a little to the east. Where is the highest concentration of the enemy?"

"Pick a direction, but I think mostly to the north."

Don directed his attention to us. "OK, boys and girls the show is about to start. Pick your target, pull up after your run, and go right back in. Make sure your guns are armed. Don't waste your ordnance. Make it all count. When you're empty, go to the south out of range under the overcast. We will join up there. They just put out some smoke, so we know where they are. Good luck."

With that, Don rolled into his run. We spread out picking our own targets. I could see people, tanks, and heavy guns everywhere. I had some tanks with troops directly in front of me, so I gave them a short burst with my cannons to make them duck while releasing two bombs on their position. As I pulled up, I could see that the bombs had hit near or on the target. I had made that run from east to west, so I decided to make my next run from west to east on the opposite side of our Marines. The smoke that had been put out was giving me a good marking of our lines, so I wanted to get as close as I could to our troops to eliminate the enemy at their front door. I would only use my cannons until I was sure I would not hit our own men. I stayed about one hundred yards out from our battle line and let all four of my cannons go to work. As I pulled up, I was receiving a lot of AA fire with some too close for comfort. I returned on my next run in the opposite direction I had just taken, letting go two napalm bombs to suppress the AA fire. I did not pull up on this run, I just jerked my plane around to my left, staying down long enough to empty my cannons on the north side of the Marines. I was taking a lot of ground fire and felt my plane shake from all the AA fire. One shell must have exploded very near my tail. I felt the stick jump and vibrate in my hands. I was sure I had taken some damage, but I was still flying.

As we joined up south of the battle area, I could see some small holes that appeared to be rifle holes in Dale's plane. Jake called telling me part of my right horizontal stabilizer (tail elevator) was missing. My stick was a little sloppy. I could feel a vibration in it, but I still had good control. Don asked if anyone had major damage other than what he had just heard. No one volunteered anything more, so Don said, "OK, let's group up and get back to the ship. I think we did a lot of damage to give our men a little breathing room. We will get above the overcast to enjoy a little sunshine on the way home. Let me know if anything changes."

This was followed by, "Good job, Blue Flight. This is Red Flight. We'll take over now to see if we can give the Marines a little more help. Any advice?"

"Thanks, this is Blue Flight. I think the enemy concentration is more to the northeast of the Marines. I think it would be a good idea to work more to the southwest and try to clear a path out for them."

A new voice popped up, "This is Romeo, forward air controller on the ground. Blue Flight, you did a good job. Red Flight, if you can clear a path to the south-southwest, I think that would be the best area to concentrate on. What is your ETA?"

"We will start our run in about two minutes." This was followed with instructions to the rest of his flight.

We broke through the clouds at about twelve thousand feet and continued our climb. The sunshine was very welcome. Suddenly I felt an increase in the vibration of my stick. I didn't have time to ask before Jake was on the radio informing me that the remaining part of my right elevator had started to come loose and was flapping more. I asked, "Don, did you read that?"

"Roger, I did. I'll throttle back to slow us down as much as I can."

I replied, "I'm going to slip out a bit to see how much control I have in my pitch. Jake, loosen up a bit."

"Roger."

The stick was shaking a lot, almost like Elvis Presley's song, "All shook up." I had to laugh at myself for even thinking that. I moved the stick back and forward and found I still had some control, but it was very sloppy. "Don, my pitch control is not good; I don't think I can land on the carrier this way."

"Max, we can try to make it to K6 (Landing strip in South Korea)."

"Not sure I should risk a landing. I don't have much control and could lose that at any time. Think I will have to eject. I just hope we can get into friendly territory before that happens. I will stay loose in case I lose all my elevator. Jake, you stay loose on me."

"Roger."

"Don, maybe we should go to a lower altitude in case I have to eject. I know you will burn more fuel there. Think you can do that and still make it back to the ship? If we can get below the overcast, it will at least let me know what's under me."

"Max, I think we have enough fuel left. I'll start a slow descent. I am sure we are still over enemy territory, so hang on as long as you can."

"Will do, I don't think I have a lot to say about that though."

"Max, we are just above the clouds now at thirteen thousand feet. I would like to hold here. We won't break out until about four thousand feet. The weather is not good there."

"OK, will you alert rescue to see if they can reach us by chopper?"

"Roger, Dale, get on guard channel. Try to get a chopper for us. Also, alert any friendly planes in the area. We may need help with cover for Max if we can't stay."

"Roger, I'm on it."

I heard Dale put out a Mayday call but lost him when they switched to another channel.

"Max, this is Jake. You just lost part of the left elevator."

"Thanks, I can feel it on the stick. I still do have limited elevator control. You get that, Don?"

"Roger."

A short time later Dale came up on the radio. "This is Dale, they are redirecting some ADs (dive bombers) toward our location. They should be with us in about fifteen minutes. Also, a chopper will intercept us before we reach friendly territory."

"Max, this is Don, want to try to get below the overcast?"

"Let's stay up here, at least they won't know exactly where we are if they can't see us. Might give me a little edge. Got any idea how far to friendly territory?"

"I would guess about ten minutes."

"Whoops, I just lost almost all of my control."

"Max, this is Jake. About eighty percent of your elevator is gone."

"Thanks, I've got the stick full back but can't keep the nose up. If I can increase my speed, the remaining part of my elevator may be more effective." My nose was down about forty-five degrees as I entered the clouds. I was up to Mach .75 (75 hundredths of the speed of sound with the speed of sound being about 750 miles per hour). The nose was coming up slowly, but I didn't want to eject at this speed. I broke out of the clouds at about five thousand feet with the nose still down about twenty degrees. I was close to Mach .8.

"Don, I'm going to try to reduce my throttle to try to get the speed down. I would like it lower when I eject.

"Max, we are getting close to friendly territory, the ADs should be here soon. Try to eject by 1,000 feet. A little higher would be even better."

"Roger, I'm at Mach .55 passing through three thousand feet. I've got the speed brakes out. Will lower my flaps now. I may lose them, but they should slow me down and pitch me up."

"Roger." Followed shortly with, "Looks like it's working."

"I'm going through twenty-five hundred feet. I'll leave at one thousand feet. Say a prayer for me."

"Good luck, I already have."

I glanced at the airspeed indicator as I pulled the curtain (a curtain you pull down over your face after you have blown the canopy off that activates and fires the seat). I was just a little over 200 knots, so I couldn't see the canopy leave, but I sure felt the seat as the rockets in it fired. It hurled me into space, booted me away from the seat, and opened my parachute. I felt a sharp pain in my back when the seat fired. I must not have been as straight up as I should have been.

I felt a huge jerk as the chute opened and drifted slowly to earth. I looked around to see if I could see any enemy soldiers. I couldn't see any under me, but I did see some vehicles about four or five miles away. Don must have seen them too. He quickly turned in that direction, giving them a quick burst with his cannons. I was thankful he had some rounds left and was hoping he had a few more.

I rolled as my feet hit the ground, tangling me in the parachute lines. I untangled the lines, stood up, and discarded my Mae West life jacket since it was bright yellow and stood out for miles. Don flew over me very low, turned toward the vehicles, and gave them another short burst of cannon fire. I was certain it was his last since it was so brief.

I started for a small stand of trees a short distance away as two AD dive bombers dove toward the vehicles, each releasing a bomb. They were both right on target. I know they couldn't hear me, but I offered them my thanks anyway.

Don passed over me at a very low altitude, gave me a salute and waggled his wings, telling me he was leaving.

The next thing I heard was a chopper in the distance. I was rather hypnotized by it until I saw dirt kicking up around me. I was receiving enemy fire. An AD passed over me at treetop level with his cannons coming to life. The area he was firing at was a small grove of trees which he literally chewed to pieces.

I heard the chopper behind me and turned around. I watched as it came in to land. The other AD passed over us with his cannons blazing the same as the first. I did not see any return fire, so I started to run, reaching the chopper in seconds, and helped in by one of the men. Another was firing a machine gun into the brush, or what was left of the brush the AD had just hit. We were in the air before I could even get strapped in. The pilot turned to me, saying, "Welcome aboard."

I just gave him the best smile I could find and returned with, "Thank you. Glad you could drop by."

The chopper took me to their base hospital, which was about 30 minutes away. They stopped long enough for me to get out. As I stepped out of the chopper, I tried to get the pilot's attention to thank him. He did see me and offered a thumbs up which I returned. He was gone in seconds.

I was escorted by two Army personnel over to what appeared to be the headquarters. I was greeted with a handshake from an officer who appeared to be in charge. He said, "Welcome to MASH (Military Army Surgical Hospital). Got any wounds that need attention? "

"Just my pride and sore back," I returned.

He pointed to a bottle on his desk. "That's our injured pride remedy. Take a shot. Also works for nerves and sore backs. We need to keep you for a few days to make sure you didn't damage something in your back. Got anything else you want me to look at?"

"Not that I know of. How do I get back to my ship?"

"We have some people that will work that out after we are sure your back is OK. We've been kind of busy, so it may take a little time. Just relax for now. This will probably hit you later. There's a cot in the next room. I suggest you lie down for a while."

Thanks."

CHAPTER II

I was starting my third day at The MASH unit. My back was still somewhat of a problem so they would not release me. The news came in that the enemy had started falling back around the Marines at Chosin. The MASH unit could expect to start receiving wounded tomorrow morning. The doctor I had been talking to said our sorties had been very effective. Taken a heavy toll on the North Koreans. I thought a while and offered, "My back is painful, but not bad enough to keep me from helping where I can. Got anything I can do to help?"

"How bad is your back?"

"I would say improved. I can try to help wherever you need me."

"We can use the help; I am sure we will be swamped when the Marines start coming in. Have you had any training in the medical field?"

"Nothing past putting a band-aid on a cut, but I will do whatever you need me to do."

The doctor smiled, looked at me and said. "If you can fly a jet, I guess we can make you more than a band-aid applier. Can you work around blood without fainting?"

"I really don't think that would be a problem."

"Good, go over to the surgical unit and ask for Danny. It's the second building that way." He said as he pointed in the direction I should take.

I just turned and left. As I entered the door of the building he had pointed to, I stopped the first guy I saw to ask where I could find Danny. He pointed to a group standing by a patient, "Over there."

My eyes turned in the direction he was pointing, but all I saw was a group of female nurses. "I need to see Danny, that's a group of girls," I argued.

He looked at me rather bluntly, "That's because Danny is a girl."

I didn't say a word, I just walked over to them, "I'm looking for Danny."

One of the girls turned to face me, "I am Danny, what can I do for you?"

For a moment, I was speechless and couldn't get a word out. I think my mouth was moving, but nothing was coming out. I just stared at the most beautiful girl I had ever seen.

She looked at me with a rather puzzled look. "Are you OK, is something wrong with you, are you injured?"

I had to clear my throat before I could answer her, even then it was barely audible. "I was told to ask for you," I said.

Her expression had turned rather sober as she said again, "What can I do for you?"

I had my courage up by this time, so I answered with a little more authority. "I was told to ask if you can use some help."

Kind of a fake smile crept across her face as she said, "That is very nice of you, Lieutenant, I see you are wearing pilot's wings, I don't happen to have any airplanes around that need flying. It was nice of you to add a little humor to our day. Thank you." With that, she turned her attention back to the other ladies.

"I'm sorry, Danny, I should have made that clearer. I was shot down a couple of days ago and ended up here. My back is still sore, so the doctor won't let me leave. I know you will be having a lot of wounded Marines coming in, I would like to offer my help if you can use it. The doctor said you could use my help here. He told me to look you up."

Danny hesitated for a short time, "We can sure use some help, I am just not sure what I could have you do. Where would you like to help?"

"Danny, I don't care if it's mopping blood off the floor. I was at Chosin and saw what the Marines have been going through. I was flying support for the Marines when my plane was hit by ground fire. I had to eject on the way back to the ship. Some of your guys in a chopper came in under enemy fire and pulled me out of a very bad situation. I just need a way to say thank you."

This time the smile was honest as she said, "May I call you by your name? I would rather do that than just call you Lieutenant."

"My name is Max, it is a pleasure to meet you, Danny."

"Thank you, Max, it is certainly a pleasure for me as well. I can certainly find something more dignified then mopping for you to help with. I do need someone to help assist the doctors in surgery. It would mostly be to help position the wounded on the operating tables to ensure a smooth and orderly flow. I can give you a short course on what you will be doing. Does blood bother you?"

"Danny, I won't allow it to bother me. I saw firsthand what the Marines were going through. They had a lot more to contend with than being squeamish about looking at blood. I can do anything to help them."

"I think you already have done a lot more than that. How did you get shot down?"

"In one of my bomb runs, I took a hit to my tail section. My elevator just fell off on the way back making me lose my up and down control. I was still in enemy territory when I ejected.   One of your choppers came in to pick me up. Some other planes held the enemy at bay for them to do so. They had their life on the line. I had bullets kicking up the dirt around me just before they landed."

"Max, you certainly qualify as a hero yourself. Perhaps we can enjoy a cup of coffee and a nice talk when things slow down here. Right now, I would like to go over a few things you should know. We could get a call at any time telling us that wounded are coming.

If not, we will meet here at 0500 tomorrow morning. We need to get rid of that dirty flight suit you are wearing and get you in some clean clothes. I will give them to you before you leave. Anything else you need will be here."

We spent the next hour going through what I would be required to do to help move the wounded into the OR with some tips on how to do it in an efficient and expedited way. Sometimes the conversation drifted to our own private lives, but not to any great depth. We just talked about where we were from and what schools we had attended. We briefly touched on our families at one point.

She was wearing a wedding ring that I had a burning curiosity about but was afraid to ask. I thought it very odd that she did not tell me about her husband. I would have thought she would have at least mentioned him. I knew that it would be best if I did not get too interested in her. It could lead to a disappointment, I was sure. Besides, I have no desire to get involved with a married lady.

As we were talking, Dr. Jim arrived. Dr. Jim is the doctor I had been talking to when I first got here. He was a tall man, his face lined with fatigue and a quiet patience. He was the Colonel in charge of this MASH unit. We had gotten to be good friends in the short time I had been here. He smiled and waved as he approached us. "Thought I would find you still here. I hope you and Danny are getting along OK. "

"I think she is trying to make a doctor out of me, but about to give up."

Danny put on one of her best smiles and offered. "Max would make a fine doctor; I am not about to give up. He starts his internship as soon as the next wounded come in. I know he will be a good addition to my surgical team."

Dr. Jim smiled and said. "Better enjoy him while you can, his commanding officer wants him back. I just talked to him on the radio."

"What did you say to him, Doc?"

"I said I did not want you flying for another four or five days. I leveled with him and told him you could, in an emergency, fly sooner. He said he would have you picked up tomorrow."

I started to say something, but Dr. Jim put up his hand, stopping me, and continued. "I told him I would like his permission for you to stay here another two or three days. I also mentioned that we were expecting a large influx of wounded in the next twelve to twenty-four hours, and you had volunteered to help. You were getting schooled on what to do now. I said that if you would not be flying, I needed you here. I thought you could make a difference. That difference can be measured in lives saved. I know he thought that I was handing him a lot of B.S., but I assured him I really wasn't. I went on that you could fly right now, but your flying would be substandard, which could, and would, mean that your life would be at risk. He said that he fully understands and agreed with me. He gave you three days. He arranged for your pickup on Monday. This is Friday, so that gives you about three days, a little short of maybe, but three days. Danny, I am going to put you in charge of Max. He is your responsibility, so put him under your wing. Now, Max, do you object to having Danny as your CO (Commanding Officer) for the next three days? It may give you a little time to get to know each other. It appears that you have a good start on that already."

"Doc, you are right. I wish I could get to know Danny better, but it is not a good idea. I'm afraid I may get to like her too much, and that would not be good. Danny is married and off limits for me. That tells the rest of the story."

Dr. Jim just turned and looked at Danny. "You didn't tell him did you, Danny? Perhaps I spoke a little too soon. Sorry, guess the cats out of the bag now. You'll just have to deal with it. Max, I can get someone else to take your hand to lead you around while you are here. Just let me know." With that, he turned and started to walk away.

I was just standing there with a puzzled dumb look on my face wondering what the Doc had just said. Danny reached over and took my hand. She looked at the Doc, smiled, and said. "I've got it handled. We won't need you anymore on this issue, Doctor."

Dr. Jim just smiled, "I thought so," and walked away.

I just looked at Danny with an even more puzzled and dumb look than before. "Will someone please tell me what is going on?"

Danny just took my hand again, smiled, and said, "Let's go get a cup of coffee; we need to talk."

I hesitate, looked Danny in the eye said. "I'm not sure I want to. I have only known you a few hours, I feel like I landed in the middle of some weird clandestine cloak and dagger situation. Are you real, or is this just a bad dream I'm having? You evidently have not been honest with me. I don't think you lied to me, but I was led to believe something that I don't even have any idea of what it is, that's the same as lying. I will admit when I first saw you, I had a feeling come over me that actually scared me. I don't think I have ever experienced anything like that before in my life. Then I saw your ring. I was devastated. How in the world could I be devastated when I just met you? I will need some time to figure that one out. Just to make it plain and simple. You are married. I don't fool around with married women for any reason, and I have no respect for any man that does. This is no doubt the shortest friendship I have ever had. I find this an excellent time to end it. You will have to find someone else to play games with, Danny, not me. I would appreciate it if you would assign someone else to help me tomorrow. I said I would help, and I intend to keep my word."

I was angry, hurt, and disappointed. I just turned and walked away. As I did, I heard Danny call my name, but I just kept going.

On my way back to the hospital tent I was staying in, I thought it would be a good idea to pick up some clothes for tomorrow. I wandered over to headquarters to see where I could find some. While I was there, Dr. Jim came in. He looked a little surprised when he saw me and asked. "I didn't expect to see you here. How did things go with Danny?"

"Could have been better."

"That doesn't sound very good. Danny is always easy to get along with. What happened?"

I hesitated for a moment. "To be quite honest, Doc, I just don't care to mess around with a married woman."

"Max, what are you talking about?" Did she tell you she was married?"

"She didn't have to; she has a ring on."

Doc just looked at me. "You made a big mistake, Max, Danny is one of the nicest young ladies you could ever hope to meet, and she is not married."

"She has a wedding ring on."

"Just stop and think, Max. As pretty as she is, with all the men that go through here, what would you expect her to do?" She couldn't get anything done with all the guys hitting on her."

"Doc, are you serious?"

"Yes, I am."

"Oh my gosh, what an idiot I am. I think she was going to tell me. I didn't give her a chance. I think I just made the biggest mistake of my life. I was rude to her, thinking she was married and willing to ignore her marriage. I don't have a thread of hope after the way I acted. I need to find her and hope she will at least allow me to apologize. I owe her that."

"Max, one of the nurses is having a birthday party at the club about now. I am sure Danny will be there. Let's go over and sing happy birthday to the birthday girl."

"I am not sure she will even speak to me."

"You will never know if you don't try. I'll even put in a good word for you."

I was willing to try anything, even if I didn't think I had a chance of getting her to understand. "I would like to go over and try to talk to her, Doc."

"Let's Go."

I was not very good company on the short walk to the officer's club. When we arrived, I was not sure I should go in. I asked Doc if he thought it would be better if he said something to her first. Doc just looked at me, opened the door, and pointed in her direction, "It's time to stand on your own two feet, Max. After you, my friend."

As soon as I stepped into the room, I saw Danny. She was talking to a couple of other people with her back to me. I hesitated only to have Doc give me a shove. "Over there, my friend."

I slowly approached Danny hoping she would turn around and see me, but she did not. I just said, "Danny."

Danny turned around with a sober face and looked at me, "Oh! Hello Max, nice that you could come to the party." She turned back away from me.

I didn't move. I just said, "Danny, will you allow me one minute of your time. It will be the most important minute of my life."

The friends she was talking to sensed something and walked away. Danny still stood with her back to me. "Danny, I want you to know what happened today. I am not sure if it was the way you looked at me, you're smile or the sound of your voice. I had a feeling come over me that I'm not sure I ever felt before. I just knew you were the kind of girl I have waited all my life for. Then I saw your ring. I wanted to leave, but somehow, I couldn't. The time we spent together today seemed so very special, I enjoyed every minute of it. I really didn't want it to stop. Later, when you took my hand saying we need to talk, I thought you were willing to cheat on your marriage, I just couldn't accept that. My angel, I thought, had tarnished wings. I knew that we could never be, but I couldn't stand the thought that you could fall from the lofty pedestal I had placed you on. You will never know how happy I was when I found I was wrong.

Danny, I hope you understand. It was the way I felt about you and knew it could never go any further. It was the disappointment that was burning inside of me. It was the love I knew I could never share with you. We have only known each other for a few hours, yet I know what I feel is real. I was wrong. I will ask you to forgive me, but you can't forgive me if you don't understand the way I perceived things to be today. We can't see into the future to know if we could get together. I can only promise you that you would never regret it

Danny, you have turned your back to me just now. I will leave quietly so I will not embarrass you. I do hope you will turn around and stop me. If you don't, I wish you the best."

I turned around to walk away when Doc yelled at me to come over and have a drink. "I will if you pay for it. I left all my money on the aircraft carrier. I didn't know I was going to stop."

I heard a voice behind me. "I can float you a loan Sailor if you promise to pay me back in a few years."

I hesitated. "It might take me a long time."

"That is what I was hoping for."

I walked over to Danny. She looked at me. "Will you take my hand now? I promise not to lie to you."

"You're not going to let me forget that, are you?"

She looked at me and smiled, "Never."

We spent some time at the club with Dr. Jim and the others. I met a lot of very nice people. Knowing what tomorrow would bring with all the wounded coming, everyone left early to get some rest. It might be a long time before they find any again.

I walked Danny back to her tent, enjoying every step. She was, as the Doc had said, one of the nicest ladies I could ever hope to meet. We talked about many things, including our families. She had a wonderful loving family. We talked about seeing each other again. We both knew that it could be a long time, but we avoided mentioning that. We had been attracted to each other the first time we met but had a difficult time knowing why. We finally decided it was meant to be and enjoy it rather than question it. We were not kids with some foolish puppy love, we were adults, who had found someone we liked. We would put it in God's hands and follow our hearts to see where it would take us.

We said an early goodnight knowing what the next day would bring. Everything had been thrust upon us so fast we agreed just to like each other until we had a chance to know each other better.

As I walked away, I stopped, looked back at Danny. She was still standing there wearing a delightful smile. I smiled back and told her I had to look once more to make sure she was real. She blew me a kiss.

CHAPTER III

I awoke to the sound of choppers. At first, I was disoriented until I remembered where I was. I realized choppers were bringing in the wounded. I looked at my clock and saw it was only 0430. They must have been able to start picking up the wounded at Chosin. That meant the North Koreans had pulled back sooner than expected. I quickly dressed in the new surgical clothes I had been given and started for the surgical center. It looked like mass chaos to me, but I was sure everyone knew what their job was and doing it. I saw Danny as I walked into the room. She just motioned me over to her and pointed to a door. "That's the scrub room, I have not scrubbed myself yet. Just go in and do what the others are doing. I'll be right in, make sure you do it right."

I wasn't sure why I needed to scrub, but I did as she had said and started scrubbing my hands. It wasn't too long until Danny came in and took the sink next to mine. I was given a quick lesson on how to scrub for surgery. Danny also told me to go to surgery room five and ask for Dr. Collins. He was expecting me. They would finish prepping me for surgery. The nurses would see that I was sterile as Danny put it. As she left, she just said, "I'll see you later."

I went to surgery room five as quickly as I could to be readied for my job. As Dr. Collins entered the room, he gave me some quick instructions. He said he would try to keep the language in a form I could understand. He offered his thanks and told me if I felt nauseous to let him know right away. He emphasized that we would have to work fast, again, offering his thanks for my helping.

Suddenly the door sprang open, a gurney with a wounded marine was wheeled in. He looked like a high school kid to me. He was sedated, so he was motionless. His right side was covered with bloody bandages. Dr. Collins removed the bandages, hesitated for a moment to survey the wound, and started to work. He spoke one word, "Shrapnel, "before he started to work. I didn't have time to think about getting sick. Dr. Collins had a nurse remove the dirty bandages, probed the wounds for metal, and started to work. I was amazed at how skillful he was and how fast he worked. The young Marine was finished, sewed up and out of there in very little time. Dr. Collins turned to me, "You're doing this like you've done it before. That young Marine will be OK. We will have to check him when we get more time to make sure I got all the junk out of him. We have to work as fast as we can to save as many lives as possible." I didn't have time to answer, another Marine was already on his way in.

This went on for over five hours with an endless flow of wounded men. It was apparent that some would not survive. I think I said a prayer for every man that went through our room. Sometimes out loud. Once Dr. Collins looked at me and said, "The prayers are as important as the surgery. Please include me and ask God to guide my hands. I pray a lot, one more prayer won't hurt."

After about five hours, we took a very welcome break. Rather short, but I know it helped all of us. This continued most of the day, followed by the doctors rechecking the men they had worked on, making sure anything missed was taken care of.

When surgery was finished, I looked for Danny. I found her still going. I felt sorry for her but marveled at the job she was doing. She had to be exhausted. I told her I would like to have a little of her time later if possible. I had one more night after this one before I went back to the carrier. I did not want to be selfish, but I wanted desperately to spend some time with her. She asked me to come over to her room later, so we could just spend a quiet evening talking. She said, "I want to know more about you. I hope you want to know more about me too."

I told her that it was at the top of my priority list. I also said, "I may still have a lot of apologizing to do. I will not be satisfied until I am completely assured that I am totally forgiven and that you will see me again. Not just once, but as many times as possible until this war is over, so we can lead a normal life. I'm not sure we can make any sense of all this, but I intend to try."

"Max, I am exhausted. Will you give me some time to rest a little? I am not even sure I can make it over to the mess to eat. I feel like I may just collapse at any time."

"Danny, I can see that. I am going over to the mess, I'll get something made up for you and bring it back. In the meantime, get a shower or whatever will make you feel better. Get comfortable and get ready for bed if you care to.

I'll spend enough time to share a little food with you, talk for a few minutes, tuck you in bed, and let you get some sleep."

"Max, please, just give me some time to rest for a while. I'll be OK. You're tired too and need your rest."

"I didn't do nearly as much as you did today, so don't argue with me. How much time do you need?"

"Max, I would like to spend some time with you."

"That's nice, but I don't care to sit here watching you sleep. I asked again, "How much time do you need, I would appreciate an answer. That is the only item open for discussion as of now. "

"Just give me about thirty minutes. I don't take orders from a junior officer so I will open any item I care to."

"Maybe you didn't realize it, but the Navy rank is two steps above the Army. That makes me in command. I don't expect it will be necessary to bring that up again. I will see you in about thirty minutes. Maybe a little bit more. I need to shower also."

"You may have to wake me up, but I'll be here, Admiral."

I was back in less than an hour with some food that was still warm. As I walked into Danny's quarters, I could see she had decided to lie down on her bed. She had her PJ's and housecoat on, but completely oblivious to the world. She did not have any covers over her. I shook her very delicately, not sure if I should wake her. She opened her eyes, smiled, then closed them again. I shook her lightly again. She opened her eyes. "Danny, I have some food for you. I will put it in your cooler. We need to get you under the covers, so you stay warm. Don't want you getting sick." I helped her sit up so I could pull her covers back. She was talking to me, but I know she had no idea I was there. She laid back down as I pulled the covers up, doing my best at tucking her in. I knew she wouldn't hear me, but I started talking to her anyway. "I saw Dr. Jim a short time ago. He told me that I was going to be picked up about noon tomorrow. There is something big going on, and they want me back. I am going to early church service." I knew she wasn't hearing me, so I just told her I would leave her a note hoping she would meet me. In the note, I repeated what I had tried to tell her. I asked her to meet me at church if she cared to. If not, I would come by to see her before I was picked up. Before I left, I walked over to her, bent down, gave her a gentle kiss, and told her I would see her tomorrow. I know she never heard, but she did smile.

The next morning, as I was getting ready for church, I was tempted to go by Danny's quarters to see if she wanted to go with me. I argued with myself for a short time, finally decided that she would see my note. If she wanted to come to church, she would. As I entered the church, I saw Danny, so I sat down beside her. She looked at me, reached over, took hold of my hand, and whispered, "I don't want you to go." I smiled and squeezed her hand.

After church, we walked over to the mess hall to have some breakfast. I asked her if she had found the food I had placed in the cooler. She said she did in the middle of the night and ate a little of it. She did not find the note until morning. "If I would have found your note last night I would have come over. Why didn't you wake me up?"

"I tried, but you were completely out of it. You were talking, but you didn't make any sense. I knew you needed the rest, so I thought I would wait until this morning."

"I wished you would have tried harder."

We spent the rest of the morning walking around and in her quarters. We talked about our families and what we wanted in life. We knew we had only just met, but we told each other that we had never felt like this before, and thought we had the start of something very special. We promised each other that we would write and, if possible, see each other again while we were in Korea. If not, we would see each other at the first possible moment when we were out of the war zone. I think we both wanted to express our feelings more but were afraid to. Perhaps because we were afraid the other one would not say it back.

As we sat there, now in silence, there was a knock on the door accompanied by a voice asking if Lieutenant Bradley was there. I acknowledged him and went to the door. "I'm Lieutenant Bradley, what can I do for you."

"The Colonel would like to see you right away. He is at headquarters."

I thanked him and turned to Danny to ask if she would go with me. She agreed, so we started for headquarters both trying to guess what he wanted. I told Danny that I probably needed to sign some papers or something like that.

When we reached the Colonel's office, I knocked and was told to come in. As Danny and I entered the room, I offer a salute which the Colonel returned and said good morning.

"I have some good news for you, Max. Your commanding officer just sent me a message saying that a hold was put on the reason he needed you back. You have five more days to recuperate before he sends a chopper for you."

"Thank you, Colonel, that is good news. I'm still available to help if you need me."

"Things have slowed down a lot, but I will keep that in mind. Danny, we will only need you on a limited basis. I will have someone call if we need you, otherwise take a little time off."

Danny smiled and said, "Thank you, sir."

We both left the Colonel's office with huge smiles on our faces. I looked at Danny, "Danny, I hope you were not joking with me. You're stuck with me for the next five days. Tell me now, so I don't get to like you too much and get pushed out the door."

Danny stopped and looked at me. I saw a smile creep across her face as she said, "I'll tell you in five days if you still want me to. Until then, be nice to me, and I may let you stay."

I couldn't hold back a smile as I replied, "I will be so nice that you may never let me leave."

After talking a bit more while looking at pictures Danny had of her friends and family, we decided to go have a cup of coffee. We had only been there a few minutes when Colonel Jim walked in and headed directly toward us.

"Danny, I have decided that you have been working so hard that you require a little R & R. I have arranged for you to spend four days in Japan. Your plane will leave in the morning with several others. They have facilities at the base in Japan set up just for that purpose. Your time there will be your own. Do as you please.

I must have had a terrible look on my face as I sat there in disbelief. Colonel Jim continued. "Max, I think you could use some R & R to help recover from your back injury.

I happen to have one more seat open on the plane with your name on it. Go to supply today and draw some Army uniforms, we are out of Navy gear to wear while you are in Japan. Come by my office later, I will loan you some money, so you don't have to sponge off Danny."

I was speechless. I looked at Danny and saw a couple of tiny tears in her eyes. I stood up, "Colonel, I don't know what to say. I want to thank you, but I am not sure that is enough." I stood there trying to speak, but nothing was coming out. The tears in Danny's eyes were now more like rivers.

Colonel Jim looked at Danny. "I thought you would be happy, Danny. I can send someone else if you wish."

Danny managed a smile and said. "Don't you dare" and fell speechless.

The Colonel just said, "I'll see you later, Max," and left.

We spent the rest of the day preparing for our departure. We were like two kids getting ready for Christmas, not sure of what we would find under the Christmas tree.

CHAPTER IV

We arrived at the airfield at about 1000 hours and found ten other people. Five women nurses, two male nurses, two infantry officers, and one doctor who would accompany us to Japan for R&R. We were instant friends and started planning some activities together. We were all happy to be away from the war and intended to enjoy every minute in Japan.

The flight was not too long, about two and a half hours, with us landing at Atsugi just after 1300 hours. A bus picked us up and took us to our quarters. Two people would share a room. Danny ended up with another nurse, I would stay with the doctor.

After settling into our rooms, we had agreed to meet at the officer's club for a drink. We were all in the same barracks, so I stopped by Danny's room to walk over with her.

It was fun to be around people who are having fun, and this had to be the perfect group. Everyone had left the war behind them in Korea. For four days, we would blank it out of our minds. We stayed at the officers' club a bit longer than intended. Some decided to continue their merriment at the club while four decided to explore the local establishments.

Five of us decided to have a leisurely meal at the club and return later for a nightcap. We could then return to our rooms, attend a movie or some other activity on the base. Danny and I chose to spend time together in a very comfortable lounge in our barracks. We could then plan what we wanted to do for the rest of our R&R time. We only had two more evenings to spend in Japan, so we wanted to spend them wisely.

In a short time, some of the others came into the lounge. After visiting a while, we decided to play some Bridge. This continued longer than intended, but it was a lot of fun. I wanted desperately to spend some time alone with Danny but was not sure of how to arrange that.

As if on cue, the doctor I was bunking with, looked up from a book he was reading and remarked. "Max, I like to sit up and read, I hope you don't mind if I stay here for a couple more hours and read. Kind of a habit of mine."

"Please enjoy your book doc, you are certainly not offending me. I think Danny and I will walk down to our room and just talk awhile. The door will be open when you decide to retire."

I just heard a quick, "Thanks."

Danny and I excused ourselves and walked to my room hand in hand. I told Danny that I felt like a teenager on his first date walking his date home.

"It really is our first real date, Max, and you are walking me home. Should I anticipate a kiss at my front door?"

"No Danny, you may not anticipate a kiss at your front door. Maybe several, but not just one."

"Ooooh, that almost scares me. I had no idea you were so brazen."

By this time, we had reached my room, I hesitated long enough to open the door, but Danny just stood there.

"What's wrong, Danny, did I say something wrong."

"No, Max."

Danny just continued to stand there looking down at the floor.

"What's troubling you? If I did or said something I should not have, please forgive me. It will never happen again."

"Max," Danny hesitated, "I am not sure what you expect of me." Another hesitation, even longer. "I like you a lot. I guess it could be called kind of a falling in love. I can't give myself to anyone until I am completely sure. That may be after marriage."

I couldn't help but laugh. "Excuse me for laughing, but I thought something was really wrong. Danny, if I thought you were that kind of a girl, you wouldn't be here. Now, may I be a little presumptuous? I promise not to make any sexual advances toward you until after we are married. I'm afraid now I have laid my intentions bare, giving away my entire plan. That was stupid of me, can you pretend that you never heard what I just said?"

"Of course I can't. It is what I wanted to hear, but we have a long time to go before we reach that place. I hope not too long, but not now."

"Then, we understand each other perfectly." I stopped, "You didn't happen to look to see if I had my fingers crossed?"

"No, were they?"

"I'll tell you later."

"I'm not coming in."

"OK, no they weren't"

"Promise."

"I promise."

The next couple of days were some of the happiest days I had spent in a long time. I had left the war behind and refused to even think about it. I knew something big was shaping up, and we would again be in harm's way. Occasionally thoughts crept into my mind, thoughts that were unwanted. I found myself trembling at times. I knew I had to prepare Danny for what could happen.

I argued with myself, finally concluding that it would not do any good to worry her. I wanted her to be happy now and share a dream with me, a dream that may not happen. I wanted to prepare her for what may happen, but I felt selfish and did not want her to worry. I would play it down and hold back some of the truth to spare her the anxiety.

I will never forget our walks in the gardens of Japan. The fragrance of the cherry trees that filled the air. The feeling of her touch that stirred my soul, her smile that brought sunshine into my life.

I wanted to tell her how much I was falling in love with her, but had the stench of war in my nostrils, and the feeling of pain as fear pierced my heart.

I tried to tell myself that the ice was thin, and I must tread lightly. I could drown, but I did not want to pull anyone else down with me. I had to decide how far I could go. Can fear make you hold back and warp your thinking? Should I reach out for the things I want most in life even though someone else could be hurt? Should I find the love and happiness I want to share with someone I love, and forget about the battles not yet fought?

The last night in Japan was the most memorable of all. The officers club was throwing a party for all the people on R&R. This was part of the usual procedure. They had treated us royally during our stay with tours, movies, and other activities. Tonight was a banquet of sorts with a band composed of anyone who had a musical instrument and was willing to play. They had the perfect nightclub atmosphere. Anything with dim lights and music would have been acceptable.

Danny and I shared a table with two other couples. To us, this was like a night out in New York City. After dinner, the band started. Everyone was invited to dance. I looked at Danny, took her hand, and asked her if she would care to dance. I warned her that I was wearing Army combat boots. She said that if I started stepping on her feet, she would stand on my boots while we danced.

If the band hit any bad notes, we did not hear them. They sounded like Lawrence Welk to us. Danny was a wonderful dancer, skillfully avoided my combat boots. I held her ever so close, not wanting to let her go. The warmth of her body and softness of her cheeks made me feel that way. I couldn't help saying. "Danny, I wish I could hold you forever and never let you go. Maybe I am being a little forward and shouldn't say something like that, but I want you to know how I feel because it is so very real to me." I think I felt the moisture of her tear on my cheek.

"Max, I can't help it either. I don't want you ever to let me go. I'm getting a feeling about you that terrifies me. I don't want you to go back to your war, I want you to stay here with me."

"One day, I will be back. For now, there are only two people in this world. That is you and me. Let me fall in love with you, Danny, and let me love you forever. I know we have not known each other very long, so don't say anything. I am afraid it will not be what I want to hear."

"Max, I don't think I need to say anything, I think it is something you should be able to feel the same as I do. I want to say it anyway. I am falling head over heels in love, and since there are only two people in the world, it must be you."

"Thank you, Danny, I think I can accept that. It will do until I receive a full clarification."

The evening ended on a beautiful note. We said goodnight knowing that we had a mountain ahead of us to climb. We agreed that we would accept our situation as it was now, but we would somehow try to build on what we had. It was a wonderful place to start.

The ride back to Korea was rather quiet. We both knew I would be leaving tomorrow, but it was not mentioned. Danny and I spent the evening together. We met Colonel Jim for breakfast and thanked him again for what he had done for us. I asked him to watch out for Danny for me, telling him that I hoped we would see each other again.

After breakfast, Danny and I caught a ride to the landing strip to wait for the chopper from my ship.

It wasn't long until we heard the chopper coming and watched as it touched down. There wasn't any doubt about who they were looking for. The chopper had my ship's name and number painted on the side. We walked over to the landing area. I told Danny not to go any closer because of the blades. I could see the tears in her eyes as I pulled her close to me. I looked at her. I just couldn't hold back any longer. "I love you, Danny."

"Me too, Max."

I started to walk toward the chopper, stopped, turned to Danny, and said. "I'll be back."

"I'll be waiting."

I had to go back to hold her just once more. I kissed her and held her tight for just another fleeting moment.

She was crying and couldn't speak. I got in the chopper and watched her as we lifted off the ground. She waved, and I waved back. I watched until she faded from sight.

CHAPTER V

The ride back to the carrier was uneventful. I wanted to ask the pilot if he knew what was going on, but I knew it would be difficult to talk with all the noise the chopper was making. I wasn't sure he knew anything about it anyway. I couldn't get Danny off my mind. I wondered if it had all been a dream. I knew that wasn't true, but it was hard for me to accept. I just didn't understand how this could have happened. I was not looking for anyone, and I didn't expect to meet anyone either. Most of all, I didn't understand how this all happened so fast. I have heard of men who were going into a war zone, meet someone, fall in love, and be married that day or the next. Maybe they thought they may be killed and were trying to grab a little happiness before that happened. I don't think that was the case with me. It could happen to me, but I am sure I was not thinking that way. There was something about Danny that just drew me to her. I wasn't really sure where this would go, but I was hoping we could find a way to make it work. I felt like I'd known Danny for most of my life. Maybe there was a thing called destiny. All I know is that I was willing to accept what happened for whatever the reason that made it happen.

We reached the carrier in good time and landed on the deck. As I climbed out, I was greeted by most of the pilots in VF-21. I almost felt like a hero with all the attention I was getting. Dr. Jim must have told my skipper about Danny because I took a lot of ribbing that I had faked my damage to go spend some time with some girl I knew. They all wanted to see a picture of her, but I told them she was mine and I wasn't sharing her with anyone, not even a picture.

It was good to see everyone again. The fighting had been light after the enemy pulled out of the Chosin area. Just then, the skipper came up, greeted me, and asked how I was. I told him I was feeling good and would not have a problem flying.

"After you get situated, come to the ready room, I'll fill you in on what we have in store for us. Take your time. Let me know when you get there."

"I can head that way right now if you wish. I'm kind of anxious to hear what it is."

"That will work for me, Max. I have a stop I need to make. I will see you there in about fifteen minutes.

On the way, I stopped by my room to see if I had any mail, then continued to our ready room.

The Skipper came in shortly after I did. As he walked toward me, he handed me a small box and said, "Congratulations."

I know I was looking a little puzzled as I accepted it from him. He said, "Go ahead, open it."

It wasn't wrapped, so I just removed the lid. Inside were Senior Lieutenant's bars. He reached out his hand to shake mine and said, "You are now a Senior Lieutenant. I took the liberty of getting you your new bars."

"Thank you, Skipper, this is a surprise and very thoughtful of you."

"You are very welcome, you earned them. You will have your own flight now. I assume you want to keep Jake. He has been promoted to Lieutenant JG. He will be your section leader unless you feel otherwise. Dale was shot down at Chosin right after you were. Don followed him down and saw the North Koreans take him prisoner. Don will have to reorganize his entire flight. We have a couple of new Ensigns coming in, you two get together and figure something out. You won't have time to fly with them, so use your best judgment. Don will need new people too; you guys figure it out with the other flight leaders. I wish you had time to get some flying in with the new people, but you won't."

"Skipper, Don and I work well together, we will figure it out with the other flight leaders."

"Good! We have a real job ahead of us, it won't be easy. I will give it to you briefly now. We have a pilot's meeting scheduled for 0800 tomorrow morning where we will lay it all out. Briefly, the North Koreans have pulled back north of the Yalu river knowing we will not attack them there. They are amassing a large number of troops. and a sizeable arsenal including tanks.

There is little doubt about what they are planning to do. We just don't know when. The key is that they must cross the river before they can attack. There are three main bridges across the Yalu that we need to destroy. Our squadron has been assigned one of them. We will lay out a plan tomorrow morning and coordinate it with the other squadrons involved. The Admiral will give us a plan. He wants our input to finalize how it will go. Get together with Don and the other flight leaders. Get your decisions made about your pilots today. I want no loose strings. I have scheduled a flight leader meeting at 1500 in the ready room today."

Without hesitation, I answered. "I don't foresee any problems. I would like to have only one inexperienced pilot in my flight if possible. I am concerned about the new pilots going into combat without a chance to fly together. I think that goes for any newly formed flight, but we will make it work. I'm going down to the wardroom to get something to eat. I'll come right back and try to find Don and Jake. We'll work it out. Thanks, Skipper, for your confidence in me."

"I do have confidence, that's why you are now a flight leader." With that, we parted.

The 1500 meeting with the flight leaders went well. I had two new Ensigns who would be assigned to me. One had some limited experience, the other was completely new. I put the one with limited experience on Jake's wing. I took the shiny new Ensign.

I had the members of my flight paged and told to report to the ready room as soon as possible. Within ten minutes they were there.

I began with, "Good afternoon, gentlemen, we are from now on a flight. You probably know each other, but if you don't, get acquainted after this meeting. I am Lieutenant Max Bradley. Jake, congratulations on your promotion, you are my section leader. I am very pleased that we will still be flying together. You will have Joe as your wingman. Joe, you have some experience, I am told you performed well. Welcome to our flight. Lee, you will be my wingman. Hang close to me. You need to get some experience under your belt. I have no doubt about your ability. You too are very welcome to our flight.

Flying and staying alive is all about discipline. When I give an order, it is to be followed immediately without question. Even if you feel it is wrong, follow it. If you can, tell me as you are reacting to that order. I know I don't have to say anything more on that. There is absolutely no deviation from this rule. We will not have time to get used to each other leisurely, so learn fast. If I see something I don't like, I will make it clear how to correct it. Accept it as being constructive, not criticism."

I continued, "If something is bothering you, it is bothering me. Don't hesitate to talk to me about anything. We must remain completely focused on the job at hand. Again, you can talk to me about anything. I don't care how big or small it is. If something affects your ability to perform, we will correct it. We will be at 100% at all times."

"I am not expecting a bunch of heroes to be flying with me. With that in mind, do not take unnecessary chances. As the old saying goes, we want to live to fight another day. Be considerate of each other's thoughts and suggestions, they may be right. Any questions or suggestions before we close this discussion?" None were offered, so I closed the meeting.

The next morning at promptly 0800 the meeting was convened. The Skipper had a couple of officers with him. I assumed they were either intelligence officers or aides to the Admiral. He began by introducing the officers with him. They were from Intelligence. He continued, "I think you all know what is going on, but I will cover it again briefly. We are certain the North Koreans are getting ready for a big push. They have amassed a large number of troops and equipment north of the Yalu River.

You all know they are doing this because they consider it a safe area since we do not go north of the river. We are going to stop them from crossing the river if possible. This means that we will need to destroy the bridges they will use. We are cleared to hit the north bank with cannons if need be. We cannot take the bridges out and suppress ground fire if we are not allowed to do so.

There are three bridges we are sure they will use. They are about fifty miles apart, so we must cover about a hundred miles. The job has been assigned to our ship and our air group. The two Panther squadrons will each hit a bridge, and the AD Dive Bombers the third. We feel a run along the length of the bridges from south to north would give us the best chance. However, the powers at the top say we would penetrate the north bank too far by making our runs in that direction. Therefore, we will have to make our runs perpendicular to the bridges. They have a lot of AA set up on both sides of the bridge so it will not be a milk run. We do have one thing we can make work to our advantage. The bridges all have deep ravines below them, so we feel it is possible to come up the ravines making the AA fire level or even down at us. Their guns are not designed to operate that way, which will make it much more difficult for their gunners.

We would prefer to use bombs, but we would have to pull up sooner to drop them. That would expose us longer. You will be equipped with six rockets. That way, after you deliver your ordinance, you can make a sharp pull up. If you can jog a bit, it would be a good idea. Try to give the AA guns on the bank a little cannon fire. That will make them duck. When they are ducking, they can't aim very well."

The Skipper hesitated for a few seconds to let what he had said soak in. He started again, "We will make only one run. We hope to catch them by surprise if we come up the ravine. A second run would find them better prepared. Get rid of all your ordinance on the first run if you can. If you cannot, fire the rest from a distance, it would be very risky to make another run.

If for some reason you can't make the first run up the ravine, flight leaders, do whatever you have to. I repeat, do whatever you have to. You can interpret that any way you so choose, and I will back you up. I'm not going to lose a pilot because of some guy in Washington sitting behind a desk who doesn't want to step on Chinese toes. Try not to shoot deep into the North Bank. However, I know that even the best pilots can become disorientated. Do we have any questions so far?"

After a quick glance around the room for raised hands, the Skipper continued, "Downed pilots, you know the drill. If you are hit and can stay in the air, try to make it to the closest friendly real estate. If one of your flight goes down, try to stay as long as you can, and get a good fix on his position. Get someone to help as soon as you can. That about covers it, gentlemen, got any questions?"

One of the flight leaders stood up and asked, "Can we expect any Migs?"

"Good question, Larry. It is possible that there will be Migs. The Air Force will have some F-86 Saber jets overhead. If someone is down, don't hesitate to ask them for help. They should have enough fuel to stay in the area longer. Anything else?"

Bill stood up, "When is this going to happen?"

"We are looking at about 48 hours. Any more questions?" None were asked. "That's it, gentlemen, we will have a schedule out as soon as we know when." With that, he left.

Everyone had their own idea of what the Skipper had just said. I thought it was clear, but I knew there were some of the details that were not yet finalized. The Philippine Sea, CV 47, that we were on was an Essex class Aircraft Carrier. We had two squadrons of F9F-5 Panther jets, one squadron of F4U Corsair prop planes, and one squadron of AD Skyraider prop dive bombers.

The schedule was posted the following day just after noon. We, VF-21 with F9F-5 Panthers, were to take bridge number one. VF-22 with the same aircraft would take bridge number two. VF-25, with AD Skyraiders, bridge number three. VF-24 with F4U Corsairs would act as a mop-up. Each squadron would use eight planes except the Corsairs which were to have twelve. We are to come in low under the radar from about thirty-five or forty miles out. We would follow the river, staying in the valley all the way to the bridges.

We were to try to spread out as much as possible to cover a larger area. Don would lead the first flight, I the second.

The first two planes in each flight would concentrate on the bridge itself. The second two were to suppress AA fire on each side of the river with cannons and rockets. If possible, use any rockets left on the bridge. We, in the second group, were to stay far enough back to allow the first group to clear the bridge before we take our shots. Each bridge would have a flight of four Corsairs coming in last to pick targets of opportunity. If the bridge was not down, they were to hit it.

The launch would start at 0600. The plan was for us to go in as a group and split up about fifty miles out from the target. Then each would take up a heading to intersect the valley about five miles from their bridge, make their turn toward their bridge and start their run. Each squadron would provide two extra planes that would accompany the group to the breakup point fifty miles out. They would replace any planes that had problems and needed to turn back.

Don and I gathered both our flights in one place to make sure everyone had a handle on the situation and knew what they were supposed to do. We went through it several times to be absolutely sure. When we were satisfied, we broke up the gathering.

I went back to my room to write some letters. My first letter was to Danny. I knew the letter would take a long time to get to her, so I wanted to get it in the mail. I'm not sure I knew how to write a romantic letter to someone I had only known for a few days. My head was still going around in circles, not sure of what had happened in those few days. It was difficult for me to understand, but the feeling I felt was real. I told her if I could see her tomorrow, it would not be soon enough.

I went on to tell her that I would be going on a mission tomorrow that could have a big impact on the war. I didn't want to tell her how dangerous it would be. It appeared to me that by the time she received this letter, the mission would be ancient history. I just said that I hoped she was praying for me, and that she will always be in my prayers. Not just now, but forever. I told her again that I could not understand how I could feel this way about her, but I knew that my feelings were real, and they would never change. I just wanted to be able to tell her every day how I feel. I did not want it to be from hundreds of miles away. If I ever got to hold her again, I would never let her go. I started to think that maybe I was getting a little too romantic and better slow down a bit. I went on with some small talk and closed telling her that I did miss her and that I did feel I was sure of my feelings.

I wrote to my parents and sister, telling them that I was doing fine. I did not tell them that I had been shot down. I knew they would worry. I did tell them that I had met a girl that I was very attracted to. I hoped they would get to meet her one day soon. I told them that she had a rather unusual name for a girl. They call her by a boy's name, Danny, but that is just a nickname. It's just a version of her real name which is Danielle. I knew they would like her as much as I do.

It was getting near dinner time, so I headed for the officer's wardroom to get something to eat. 0600 would come early tomorrow morning, so I wanted to be fully rested for our mission.

Before I went to bed, I said some special prayers. I hoped I would be here to say them the next night. I asked God to forgive me for what I would have to do and to bring me back home safely. I had a very special prayer for Danny.

Surprisingly, I had a good night and slept well. When my 0500 alarm went off, I got up and started getting ready for the day. I knew the first thing I had to do was prepare myself mentally. The best way I knew how to do that is in a prayer asking for God's help. I knew I may need a lot of help the next day, so I kept that in mind as I prayed.

I prayed for all the pilots who would be on this mission. There would be thirty-six planes on this mission, so that would mean there would be thirty-six pilots. I wondered how many would be coming back and how many would be injured. A lot of men on the ship would be involved in a job that was also very dangerous. They also occupied a place in my prayers.

We are taught to hate our enemies, but few stop to think that they too have loved ones who will cry for them. Families will be left fatherless on both sides. I didn't want to go into battle. I was sure my enemy didn't either. That has somehow been a mystery to me. Why do we do another man's bidding when he does not stand in front to lead the way. If that was a requirement, for the leader to lead the battle, most battles would never occur. They would find another way. It is kind of summed up in this little verse. "Theirs's is not to reason why, theirs's is just to do and die."

After breakfast, I went to our ready room. This, in some way, is like a ball game. It is necessary to get your players in the right frame of mind for the upcoming event. I guess it's a pep talk, preparing the mind for things to come.

I knew I had to walk in there with an air of confidence to instill confidence in my men. Sometimes it is like putting on a mask, trying not to let them think of what is real.

I knew my new wingman Lee would be uptight. He was very young with no combat experience. I wished it were possible for me to put him on the sidelines and tell him just to watch this one, but he will have to learn the hard way. It will be up to me to try to keep him safe. That can also backfire on me.

I could see Lee was actually shaking. I knew I had to say something, so I walked over to him, put my hand on his shoulder, and said. "Tiger, just stick with me, I'll get you back safe. I think this will be a milk run. They don't know we're coming, and we don't intend to stay long. We should be in and out before they get their pants on. You and I are carrying the ball, Jake and Joe will run interference for us. Don't worry what is going on around you just concentrate on the bridge.

It is better to shoot a little low then high and miss the bridge entirely. You try for a column just under the bridge, and I will try to take out a span. Jake, you know what to do, make sure Joe knows also. Anyone have any questions or thoughts? Anyone unsure of his job?" The silence remained unbroken, so I wished everyone good luck and closed the meeting.

I could see Lee had settled down a bit, but I think he needed a little more assurance. I purposely looked away from Lee and at Jake. "Jake, we're in a pretty good slot, you know. Don will be ahead of us so he will draw the first fire.

After he passes, we will already be in front of the gunners and moving out of range, so they will logically move to the Corsairs behind us and shoot at them. When we have completed our run, everybody join on me, and we will head for home. If you still have a rocket, tell me, and I will decide what to do with it."

The Skipper walked into the room. He informed us that he would be in the air and be, so to speak, the Big Boss. He would oversee the operation calling the plays if any were needed. We were to go about business as usual unless he changed it. He reviewed the operation briefly to make sure everyone had it straight.

We didn't have to wait any longer, the speaker came on announcing that the pilots should man their planes.

The takeoff order would be for the Skipper to go off first on a catapult so he would be in a position to direct the operation. We would follow on the catapult with the prop planes being last making a takeoff run.

The sun was just making its presence known by peeking over the horizon. The carrier had already turned into the wind and was increasing speed preparing for the launch. The Skipper's and Don's plane were on the catapults with the jet deflectors (Barriers behind the planes) up so the jet blast would not affect the other planes behind them. It didn't take long for the pilots to be in their planes starting their engines.

Most of the other jets were parked on the deck with their tails pointing outboard so the jet blast would not affect the men and planes behind them. Jet blast can be very strong and push a man around with the possibility of being blown into a prop or over the side of the ship.

Working on the flight deck of an aircraft carrier is one of the most dangerous jobs in the world. Contrary to what many believe, pilots are not alone in a dangerous job, all the deck people on an aircraft carrier are at risk during flight operations.

The jets were quickly hurled into the sky by two catapults and a well-trained crew. The AD and F4U prop planes followed by making a run down the deck. We now had thirty-seven planes in the air, including the Skipper. The standby planes, one Panther and one AD, were not launched. If all the other planes got off, it was decided it was not necessary. Don had joined on the Skipper with his flight. The Skipper would not take part in the attack. His job was to coordinate anything he felt needed to be done.

When the other planes dropped down to stay under the radar, he would hold his position, timing it so as not to give the other planes away. He could see the river from his altitude. Therefore, he could time it to be in the right place at the right time for him to make any corrections he felt necessary. Until then, radio silence would be maintained unless it was absolutely necessary to break it. If it was necessary, it should be done wisely and quietly, so as not to let the enemy know where we were or what we were doing.

When the time came to drop down, the skipper signaled Don. Don started down with the rest of us following. As we were descending, the flights separated, taking up a heading to intersect the river at their position to turn up the river. We had a visual on the river before we started down, so we had a good bearing to follow. Due to the different distances each had to cover, we would not all reach our target at the same time. This was considered acceptable.

Don leveled out at five hundred feet, avoiding any military installations. It did not take long to reach the river. Don slipped into the valley and signaled his pilots to spread out. I lagged behind to allow for the necessary spacing. At three hundred knots, it would only take a few minutes to get there.

We were able to get in undetected. Don was at his target before they could start shooting. His section pilots (numbers three and four in the formation) were doing a good job suppressing the AA guns on each bank. They had time to release a couple of their rockets at the bridge. Don was receiving heavy fire as he pulled up to clear the bridge. There was too much smoke and dust to see where Don and his wingman had hit before we were in a position to fire. It was our turn now. The AA had increased, but the gunners were having difficulty shooting at us because we were close and at a low angle. Jake and Joe were very effective in making them keep their heads down.

Nevertheless, we were now receiving heavy AA fire. I released all six of my rockets and jerked the stick back. As I did, I felt my plane shudder as a shell exploded where I would have been if I would not have pulled up. I knew I had some damage.

I looked over for Lee but did not see him. Jake and Joe joined up on me. I still did not see Lee. I did see we had hit the bridge, but I didn't know how bad. The Corsairs were just clearing the bridge. I could see one was trailing smoke. I again looked for Lee, but he was not in sight. I looked over at Jake, who was on my left wing. Jake just looked at me, giving me a thumbs down. My heart sank. Jake was telling me that Lee didn't make it.

Skipper broke radio silence with. "Good job guys, you did a lot of damage. Come join on me, let's go home."

Jake knew radio silence was no longer in effect. "Max, Lee was hit or flew into the bridge. When I saw him at the bridge, he was on fire and went into the river right after."

"Are you sure, Jake?"

"I'm sure, Max."

I had a very difficult time accepting what Jake had just said. I blamed myself. Maybe I didn't watch him close enough. I must have done something wrong. I could see him this morning when I tried to build his confidence. Should I have done that? I said a prayer and tried to shut him out of my mind. I knew that was impossible, he would never leave, he would be there forever.

I know I was trembling. I keyed the mic. "Jake, you and Joe OK?"

"I'm OK, Joe took a hit to his left wing. He lost his wing tank. It was empty, so it didn't cause a fire. You have a hole in the bottom of your fuselage. I'm surprised your engine is still running. Must have been at the right angle to miss your engine."

"I knew I had taken a hit. Everything seems to be running OK."

I could hear other pilots talking. We had lost several planes and a lot with damage. The Corsairs had been the last ones in and received more than their share of damage and losses. I hoped we would not have to go back again. That was the worst AA I had ever seen. At times all I could see ahead of me were AA bursts. It had to be a wonder that any of us were still alive.

The skipper was on the radio asking for damage reports by flights. We had to make sure we got every plane back on the ship we possibly could. That meant that the damaged planes that could stay in the air would be last, so they didn't foul the deck, making it difficult for others to be able to land. If some were bad enough, they would have to ditch in the sea. It may even be possible to divert a damaged plane to a nearby friendly field. If my hook came down, I would be OK. If not, I would have to go into the barriers on the ship.

From the reports the Skipper received, we had lost four planes with one pilot ejecting. We were so low the others could not eject. We think Lee may have flown into the bridge. The other two had to ride their plane down. One pilot was seen running away from his plane, the other plane exploded on contact with the ground.

We had two in the air that would probably not make it back to the ship. They would try to get to friendly territory before ejecting. The nearest friendly airstrip was too far away to try for. Three more of the planes had pilots with injuries. They would have to land first, so they could get medical attention. So far it appeared that no one would have to ditch. This was very welcome. Ditching at sea is risky. The plane will often flip over when the nose contacts the water. The pilot must have his cockpit open so he can escape after he is in the water. There is a chance he will be rendered unconscious if the plane flips.

It has been a costly day for us. We lost four planes and two pilots that we were reasonably sure of. Two more pilots were on the ground and would certainly be taken prisoner. Two more planes would not make it back to the carrier. We've lost six planes and two pilots with at least two more being taken prisoner. We still had to deal with getting damaged planes back on the carrier.

The Skipper came up on the radio giving us a report of what he saw. He said we hit all three bridges successfully. He wasn't sure all three were down. He saw that the one to the west had both its spans fall. He was not sure about the other two. He did know that the bridge in the middle had at least one of its spans down.

The rest of the way back to the ship was rather quiet. The pilots in the two badly damaged planes ejected over friendly territory and would be picked up by chopper. The landings back at the carrier went well with some planes going into the barriers. My hook came down, so I was alright. The two wounded pilots were taken straight to sickbay.

Now, all we had to do was wait for the report on the bridges.

CHAPTER VI

The report on the bridges reached us the next day. Two of the bridges were completely down with the third, the middle one, having one span still intact with the other span only partially down. They needed to wait to see how fast they would repair it. If it looked like they would get it back in use in a short time, the bridge would need to be hit again. That would be something none of us were looking forward to doing.

The fighting since the attack on the bridges had been light, making our job easier. For the next several days we flew only a few sorties with only light resistance. The enemy had been working on the damaged bridges. They were also starting to construct a temporary bridge to replace the two we destroyed. It was clear that we would have to go back and hit both the repaired bridge and the new temporary one they were building. If we could only hit the troops and equipment on the other side, it would make it easier and do a lot more good. It was difficult to understand why we could not fight the war the way we should without having our hands tied. We knew the Yalu River was the dividing line between the Chinese and Korean cultures. If the equipment was coming from China, why couldn't we hit it? Everyone knew the Chinese were in this war. I guess it was a pretend war. If we pretended we didn't know the Chinese were involved, they would pretend they were not. It cost American lives. That was our government betraying our people. It was like a big game with the chips being human lives.

We finally got the word. We would hit both bridges again. This time we would also concentrate on the weapons. Mostly the AA on the south side of the river. It was the same story, different version. We hit the southside while we let them shoot at us from the northside. The United States would just throw in a few more chips, which were human lives. We would carry four five hundred-pound bombs and be able to come in from the south to bomb the length of the bridge. We were told to pull up on the northside as soon as we could. One of my friends remarked, "Guess they want to let them have a better shot at us."

The mission was scheduled to go down in two days. They would have the schedule and the rest of the particulars the next day. We had talked among ourselves and decided if we would stay down in our run just a few seconds more, we could get off some cannon fire at the gun emplacements to make them keep their heads down a little longer, that would help the guy behind us. Someone remarked that they may court martial you and put you in front of a firing squad. Someone said that they already were, only they were using North Koreans for the firing squad. It was a mission we would not be looking forward to, but we knew it had to be done.

I still had Lee on my mind and asked the Skipper to let me write the letter to his parents. I still had a lot of guilt.

I told the Skipper we should not have put him in such a dangerous mission for his first one. The Skipper made a lot of sense when he said, "Max, that wouldn't help. When you make a run like we did, even if you have a hundred missions under your belt, they are made the same way with the same guys shooting at you with the same weapons. It could have been any one of us, no matter how much experience we had."

"You know, Skipper, I never stopped to think about that. Any one of us could have been in his airplane. Nothing would have changed. I guess what is so hard to accept is that he was so young with so much life yet to live. I would like to write to his parents if it is OK with you?"

"I think his parents would appreciate it if you would, Max. Let's just add it to mine. I do have that obligation, but I know yours would mean a lot to them."

I retired to my room and penned a letter to Lee's parents. I never was able to get to know him well, but I knew what they wanted to hear about their son. I told them with honesty what I knew and how he had died. I knew it would be hard for them to accept the loss of their son, but I wanted them to know that I felt he was a very brave man.

Later that day, in our ready room, a list of pilots was posted giving the names of eight pilots who were to report to their ready room at 0800 the next morning. There was little doubt about the job ahead for the pilots on the list. It included Don, his flight, and my flight. The names in my flight included myself, Jake, Joe, and a new one, Ltjg. Chris Wallace. I had met Chris; he had been in one of the other flights that had broken up due to losses within that flight. I had Chris paged and told him to report to our ready room.

Chris was there in just a few minutes. When he came in, I shook hands with him and told him it looked like he would be my new wingman. It was also apparent that we would fly the next mission on the bridges. I was immediately impressed with Chris and the way he appeared. He had a good handle on his job since he had been doing it for a couple of months.

His confidence level was high, with a determination to do his job well. I did cover all the basics of what I expected and how we would work together. I was sure we would be one of the flights to hit the bridges on the Yalu River. He had been on the first mission, so he was aware of the risks that we would be taking. I told him to be at the meeting in the ready room at 0800 the next morning.

I left and went back to my room. I had some letters to finish and a book I had started to read.

The next morning after breakfast in the Officers Wardroom, I went to our ready room. It wasn't long until the Skipper appeared with an Intelligence officer for the briefing. The rest were there, so we started. It was explained to us that they wanted the best pilots to be on this mission, so that is why we were picked. I wondered if they were trying to build up our egos. Chris had been selected as my wingman because of his experience, and he was just plain good. I could not have been happier with that bit of news. I couldn't help but wonder how many of us would come back. They were going to send eight of us into an inferno. I didn't even want to know what the chances were of any of us coming back. The logical action would have been to attack the troops and equipment they had on the north side of the river, but that was off limits. It was common knowledge that the Chinese and Russians were behind all this and supplying the equipment to the North Koreans. We knew it, they knew it, as well as everyone in the world knew it.

They were afraid that the Chinese and Russians would enter the war, and no one bothered to admit they already were. We should call them on it and fight the war with the knowledge and ability we have. They are making a fool of us, and now they are telling me that I may die so some big shot in Washington will not have to apologize to an enemy we refuse to call an enemy.

My thoughts were interrupted when the Skipper started to speak. "This will not be an easy mission, gentlemen. You have a very heavy task ahead of you. Max, your flight will hit the old bridge. Don, your flight will be assigned to the new bridge they are constructing over the river. We know they have built up the defenses around both sights so it will not be easy. We have been cleared to hit our targets along the length of the bridges, which will give us a higher degree of accuracy. You will be pulling up over the north bank of the river which has a high concentration of AA fire. That will, no doubt, be the most dangerous part of your attack."

I interrupted, "Skipper, if we stay down longer to get past the guns and throw some cannon fire at them, we would have a better chance. If we make an immediate pull-up, we will be exposed to every AA gun within a quarter mile."

"I know, Max, this isn't my idea. We just can't go too deep into Chinese territory without causing a backlash from China and Russia."

"Skipper, you may be sending some of us to our death because we can't take the precautions we need to. Don't tie our hands, give us a chance to at least come back alive."

The Skipper turned away from the pilots and looked at the wall behind him. He stood there for a long time. There was not a sound from any of the pilots. You truly could have heard a pin drop. He slowly turned around.

"Do whatever you have to, Max, just come back alive. That is an order and one I will back up one hundred percent." No one spoke. The Skipper continued, "Don, you are relieved as flight leader. I will lead your flight. You drop back to section leader and let one of the younger wingmen be relieved." The silence continued with only Don offering a feeble, "yes, Sir."

I was stunned. I didn't want the Skipper to go on this mission, but I felt good that one of the younger pilots would be relieved.

The rest of the particulars were discussed before we closed the meeting. The usual about downed pilots and what rescue would be in the area was discussed. We were told we would each have four five hundred-pound bombs. We would have only one chance to drop them. There would not be a second pass made.

I did not like it that the Skipper had decided to go. I did not want to see anything happen to him, but this did relieve a young man from a very dangerous mission. We were told to be in the ready room at 0500 the next morning.

It was very quiet as everyone left the ready room. I am sure a lot of letters would be written. I was no different. I decided to write to Danny. The mission would be over before she received the letter so she would not have to worry about it. I would have liked to talk to the Skipper, but I wasn't sure what I would say. I felt it was better this way. We would have an experienced pilot while a younger pilot was relieved of what may have been his last flight. There isn't any way you can feel good about any part of this mission.

I went to bed early knowing sleep would be difficult to find. I said a lot of prayers hoping they would be a catalyst to bring us all back safely. I also, again, prayed for my enemy and their families. I knew that the next day's action would bring forth a lot of sadness that would be born upon wings that would deliver it to many places and many people. A sadness that would last forever and never be understood. There will always be the haunting question of why this happened, and there will be no acceptable answers.

The night was very restless for me, it seemed I would wake up every few minutes and see the bridge in front of me. This went on for half the night before I did drift off into a deep sleep. I was awakened at 0430 and reminded that I had to be in the ready room at 0500.

I stopped by the wardroom to grab some coffee. I knew I couldn't eat, my stomach was churning, making me feel a little sick. I knew it was the flight coming up that was causing it, so I tried to ignore it as best I could. I think everyone was worried about this flight and wondering if they would be coming back. I don't think there could be anything said to make anyone of us feel better. This would be the toughest mission any of us had ever flown.

The skipper went through all the basics about the flight to make sure everyone would do his job the way it was planned. Any slip-ups could be fatal for someone. The word finally came down for the pilots to man their planes. There was not a big rush to the flight deck, just a casual pace. It appeared that no one was in a hurry to go on this mission. Everyone was fully aware of what was ahead of them. Jake came up behind me and started to walk with me. "Max, I have a funny feeling about this mission." He hesitated as though he was having a hard time speaking. He began to speak again with a rasp in his voice, "you know me better than anyone in the squadron. If I don't make it back, will you write to my parents?"

"We are all coming back, but I would write to them, you know that. Would you do the same for me?" I asked.

"Of course."

We reached the flight deck and started for our planes. As we came to Jake's, I stopped, took hold of his shoulder, and said. "Jake, think positive, don't let anything else creep into your mind. Keep your mind occupied with what you are doing. That will keep the negative thoughts out."

"I'll do that, Max. Good Luck."

"Good luck to you too, Jake." I didn't say anything to Jake, but I had a bad feeling about this mission also. I felt sure all of us would not return. I just didn't want to think about it.

The sun was starting to make its appearance with little arrows that seemed to herald its arrival. As it rose further into the sky, the arrows seemed to grow larger as the sun burst forth in all its glory.

The takeoffs looked good. We joined up and proceeded in formation, maintaining radio silence, trying not to be detected. I knew it would take close to an hour to get to the target, so I decided to say the rosary. Somehow, I knew that would give me added strength and courage.

As we continued in a cloudless sky, I thought what a beautiful day, perhaps a beautiful day to die. I reprimanded myself, telling myself that I had just told Jake to think positive thoughts. I thought that I will change that to a beautiful day to live. Danny was dominating most of my thoughts. I was wondering how fast all this had gone and wondered if it was only a dream. How can anyone fall for someone in only a few days? One can't be sure until you get to know someone better. I thought that I wanted it to be real, and it would be real in my mind, and I would make it real in my life. I knew she had to be the one, I just couldn't feel this way without being sure that there were special attractions and destiny that brought us together. A chill came over me as I thought that, if I didn't get back, it wouldn't make any difference. I just couldn't let that happen.

As we neared the point, we would each take up the heading to our target, I waved at Skipper and pointed in the direction I was going to take. Skipper just gave me a thumbs up and saluted me. I returned the salute and offered him a thumbs up. We both altered our heading in the new direction. I wondered if he was thinking the same as I, wondering if we would ever see each other again. I reprimanded myself and reminded myself again to think positive.

We were only about a hundred miles out. At 300 knots we would cover that distance in about twenty minutes. Chris was on my port (left) wing, Jake was a little further out on my starboard (right) wing with Joe on his starboard wing. I started letting down continuing to keep my airspeed up all the way to the target. I knew we would not be able to jog around to throw the gunners off. We would be going in fast, remaining on a steady course. We had to do this to give us more accuracy when we released our bombs.

I signaled for everyone to get in a trail position. We would stay close behind the man ahead of us, staying out of his slipstream, (the turbulence the plane leaves as it passes through the air) to keep the gunners from having time to shift their fire from one plane to the next. I would be the Judas goat, having the gunners concentrate on me because I would be the first in.

I could see the bridge ahead of me, I armed my bombs and continued to bore in at a high rate of speed. They had time to get to their guns as I knew they would. They were already sending up some gunfire that was bursting in front of us. I released all four of my bombs before I even reached the bridge, knowing it would take them a while to get to the bridge at the speed I was going. I kept my altitude at under a hundred feet to increase my accuracy. The others would have to stay up a little to avoid my bomb blasts and pieces of the bridge. Shells were bursting all around me as I went even lower. I was very low as I passed over the guns on the north bank. I was touching off my cannons at anything in front of me. If I didn't kill them, I wanted them to duck. They cannot shoot when they are ducking. I stayed down well past the enemy guns, amazed that I had not been hit by ground fire. As I pulled up out of range of the guns, I started a slow turn to port and could see the bridge. The bridge had been reduced to rubble. We had done our job.

As I watched, Chris slipped into formation on me. He had lost the wing tank and part of his starboard wing. He looked at me and gave me a thumbs up indicating he was able to stay in the air. Jake pulled into position on my other wing with a thin trail of fuel leaking from the bottom of his plane. I could see numerous holes in his wing and fuselage. He saw me looking around for Joe and just gave me a thumbs down. He was telling me Joe didn't make it.

I came up on the radio. "What happened to Joe?"

Jake answered. "I didn't see him until I was pulling up. He must have gotten hit (Jake paused) over the bridge. His plane was hit on the north side. (Jake paused again, his voice shaking with emotion.) He could not have survived." I knew Jake was having difficulty talking. His voice was breaking up as he would stop, regain his voice, and try to speak again.

"Jake, you are leaking fuel, what is your condition?"

"The plane is handling OK, but I have a noise and vibration that I am sure is in the engine."

"Chris, what is your status?

"Everything is running, and the gauges look good. Handles a little odd with part of the wing gone."

"Watch your fuel gauge, Jake. I am going to buster, (go at full speed) so you can use as much fuel that you can before you run out. Keep me posted on your state (the amount of fuel left). I hope we can make it back to the ship before you use all your fuel. You may have to eject if you do run out. We don't have a friendly airfield near enough for us to make it to. Chris, let me know if anything changes."

I received two "Rogers" in return. I advanced the throttle as far as I thought I should and waited for anything from either Jake or Chris. Chris was the first. "Max, I am getting a lot of vibration in my starboard wing."

"Roger Chris, how are you standing up, Jake?"

"I'm going good, only a little vibration in my engine."

"Roger that, Jake. Chris, I will try to give Skipper a call to see if you can go back with them. I heard them on the radio, so they should be near us. We need to keep our speed to get Jake back before he runs out of fuel." I heard two clicks of the mic from Chris. He was telling me he heard me.

I put out a call on the guard channel (the channel that broadcasts on all channels). "Blue leader, this is Red leader, over."

Almost immediately, I heard back. "This is Blue leader, over."

"Skipper, this is Max. I have one plane losing fuel. I need to get him as close to the ship as I can before he runs out. I have another with damage and can't keep up with us. Can he tag on to you and go back with you?"

"Sure thing, go to channel one zero, so we can get off guard channel."

I switched to channel ten and knew Jake and Chris had heard the Skipper and would switch to channel ten also. "This is Blue leader, you got a copy, Max?"

"Got you loud and clear."

The Skipper continued, "Chris, I'll give you a long count (counting from one to ten) so you can bird dog (radio direction finder) me." That followed with a long count for

Chris. After a few seconds, Chris acknowledged that he had the direction to the Skipper and turned toward him.

I came up on the radio. "Skipper, what kind of shape is your flight in?"

"We all took hits but are still in the air. My wingman has some personal injuries and is fighting to stay conscious. I am trying to get to friendly real estate so he can eject before he does pass out. This is a tough call. I am trying to keep him talking. If he goes now, he will be taken prisoner and probably won't survive. We will be over friendly real estate in a few minutes. We will slow down after he goes so Chris can catch us. We could use a couple prayers."

"You got them, good luck. Take care of Chris for me."

"Will do, get Jake back in one piece." With that, he turned his attention to his injured wingman. The wingman acknowledged the Skipper, so that was good news.

I made a quick call to Jake telling him to switch to channel nine, so we would get off the Skipper's frequency and allow us to talk. I asked Jake for his state. He returned, telling me he still had 1500 pounds (jet fuel is always measured in pounds, not gallons). That told me the leak was not as bad as I thought. We continued at buster speed. I was concerned that the leaking fuel could ignite, so I called Jake. "Jake, there is a possibility that the leaking fuel could ignite, be prepared to eject at the slightest indication. If I see something, I will just say eject. It's your call if you want to go at any time. I will stay with you."

"Roger, Max, I think I will take my chances for now."

I took the time to look around and scan the sky around us. I was startled when I picked up two planes at ten o'clock high. "Jake, we have two bogies (unidentified aircraft) at ten o'clock high. I can't tell what they are. I know they are not Panthers because they don't have end wing tanks. I am going to guard channel to see if we have any Airforce F-86 Saber jets in the area." I switched to the guard channel and put out a call for any F-86 Sabers south of the Yalu river to identify themselves.

In a short time, I heard. "This is Bouncer, we are just south of the Yalu with four Sabers."

My heart sank, I knew now we had two Mig 15 jets above us. "Bouncer, this is Max, we are two Navy Panthers with two Mig 15 jets above us. I am escorting a damaged plane back to the carrier. We are about 150 miles south of the Yalu and moving away from you at high speed, so I don't think you can help us."

"If you turn back toward the Yalu, we will get to you as fast as we can. That should only take a short time."

"Bouncer, my damaged plane is losing fuel, so I can't do that without losing him. Guess you'll have to sit this one out. If you head this way, there is a chance you could help, but very little."

"Navy, give me a count so I can get a direction on you, we can at least try."

I did give him a count and told him I was going back to channel nine. He said he would be on nine also. I could see the Migs moving into a position for an attack. "Jake, keep your speed up. I don't know if you can do much evasive maneuvering with your damaged engine. They are starting a run on us.

Break away from them when they are ready to shoot. I will do a loop and try to scare them away or get on their tail. They could come after me, but it should throw them off. We just must play it by ear. If I can, I will call a break (hard turn just before they shoot to throw them off) for you. We are not a match for the Mig, but we may get lucky."

"Got it, Max, I see them. Let's just do what we have to do."

I pulled up hard and went into a loop. I cut my throttle at the top to slow down and turn tighter, then increased it on my way down. One Mig continued in his run on Jake, the other turned toward me. I lost sight of Jake, trying to concentrate on my Mig. My Mig saw he was not going to get a shot at me, so he started into a loop after me. That slowed him down, and my speed had increased on the downward side of the loop.

I followed him into another loop and gained on him. As we hit the top of the loop, we both were inverted and slowed down, but I had closed on him enough to get a shot at him. I squeezed off a full two-second burst from my cannons. I could see my tracers on a path that lead directly into him. He tried to roll out on the downward side of the loop, but I was still behind him. I just rolled out with him. He was directly ahead of me and at close range and in a vertical dive. I squeezed the trigger again and saw him blow up, sending debris in all directions.

I had been too intent on my Mig and did not know the other had followed me. As I pulled up, I saw tracer bullets flying past my canopy and felt a jar as others tore into my plane. My engine started coming apart, I lost control as I entered an uncontrollable spin. For some reason, I had not exploded, but I knew I had a fire, and part of my port wing was gone. I think the fire must have gone out, but I was still in a spin and could not recover. At about 10,000 feet for some reason, the airplane recovered itself but was still in a forty-five-degree nose down dive. I tried to take control back, but the plane only gave me a partial response. I stayed with it to about 4,000 feet but knew it was futile. I hit the pre-ejection lever which blew the canopy off and armed my seat. I took a deep breath and pulled the ejection curtain down over my face. I felt the jolt as the rockets under my seat propelled me skyward.

My chute opened, forming a beautiful white umbrella above me. I floated effortlessly toward the earth like a feather gently swinging back and forth. My serene feeling soon vanished when I saw what was below me. There to greet me were vehicles with soldiers pouring out of them. I would land right in the middle of what appeared to me to be the entire North Korean Army. Suddenly it occurred to me that they just may shoot me as I floated toward the earth. That sent a little chill up my back. I had a lot of guns pointed at me. It only took one guy to decide to pull the trigger.

When I hit the ground, I fell backward with the chute starting to drag me on my back. I had my hands over my head, hoping they would take that to mean I was surrendering. Some of the soldiers grabbed the chute to stop it. I just lay there, not daring to move. A soldier came up to me, motioning with his rifle for me to stand up. When I did, he removed my pistol and knife that I wore on the leg of my flight suit. He pointed in the direction of a truck and prodded me with his rifle. I started walking with my hands on my head. When I reached the truck, one of the soldiers hit my back with the butt of his rifle, causing me to fall to the ground. Immediately, what appeared to be an officer gave the soldier a real tongue lashing. The soldier came to attention grunting something I could not understand. The officer walked over to me, in good English told me, I was now a prisoner of war. I just stood there saying nothing.

After a lot of conversation among the officers, I was tied with my hands behind my back and escorted to an open truck. I was helped in and motioned to sit down on the bed of the truck. Several soldiers sat around me with their guns pointed right at me. Nothing was said as we drove away.

We drove for about an hour before we came to a stop. I was then removed from the truck and marched to a building that was flying the North Korean flag. I was taken to a dark room with one light and made to sit down at a table. My hands were left tied behind my back, making it very uncomfortable to sit in the hard-wooden chair. I sat there for about a half-hour before I heard someone open the door and walk in. From the insignia he was wearing I assumed he was a Major or whatever they called a Major.

"Good afternoon, welcome to North Korea. You can have a nice stay if you cooperate with us or one not so nice if you do not."

"My name is Max Bradley; I am a Lieutenant in the United States Navy. My serial number is 570910."

"Thank you, Lieutenant, but I will require a little more information than that if you intend to have a nice stay with us."

"My name is Max Bradley; I am a Lieutenant in the United States Navy. My serial number is 570910."

"Lieutenant, tell me the name of your ship, the number of planes on it, and your squadron."

"My name is Max Bradley; I am a Lieutenant in the United States Navy. My serial number is 570910."

I felt a blow to my back with some sort of a club, maybe a heavy rope wrapped in tape. It knocked me out of my chair and on to the floor.

I was helped back up and told to sit on the chair again. "Lieutenant, I asked you a question, and I would like an answer. Do I need to repeat the question again?"

"My name is Max Bradley; I am a Lieutenant in the United States Navy. My serial number is 570910."

Again, I felt the club, but with more force. I again fell to the floor while trying to catch my breath. I was afraid they had broken my shoulder blade, but I was not about to whimper and give them any satisfaction. I was again helped to the chair.

The Korean officer looked directly into my eyes and said. "Lieutenant, I will put the question to you one more time. If you do not answer, you will be taken out and shot. Can I make that any clearer? Lieutenant, tell me the name of your ship, your squadron and the number of planes on the ship."

"My name is Max Bradley; I am a Lieutenant in the United States Navy. My serial number is 570910."

I was repeatedly struck with the club until I lost consciousness.

CHAPTER VII

I could hear my name being called. Everything was a blur, and my head was spinning like a child's top. Slowly I focused on someone standing over me and calling me by name. When my vision cleared, I bolted to an upright position. Standing over me was Lee, my wingman who I thought was killed the first time we hit the bridges on the Yalu River. I knew I must be dead. If I could see Lee and he was dead, I must be dead also. I just stared at Lee and said. "Lee, your dead, am I dead too?"

"You're not dead, Max, nor am I. We are both in a Korean prison camp."

I still had a puzzled look. "You hit the bridge and exploded, Jake saw you hit the bridge and go into the river."

"I didn't hit the bridge; I took a hit right over the bridge and lost control. I went into the water which put the fire out. They were waiting for me as I crawled out of the river. I didn't have a chance to run, they would have shot me. What happened to you?"

"We hit the bridges again. The ground fire was unbelievable. I made it through OK, but Jake was hit and was losing fuel, so I was escorting him back when two Migs jumped us. I got one, but the other one got me. I ejected, but the entire North Korean Army was waiting for me. They worked me over when they tried to interrogate me, I'm not sure I don't have something broken. They beat the crap out of me."

"Ya, Max, they do that with everyone. They seem to get tired of it after they figure out they can't get you to give them any information. No doubt they will have a go at you a time or two yet. Just keep your mouth shut, and they will give up."

"What do you do all day, Lee?"

"They do make us work sometimes, but that is reserved more for the enlisted men. The officers are treated a little better. They are trying to make you think they know we are using some sort of germ warfare. They are constantly after you for a confession. I have heard they have used some torture methods, but so far none of us here have had to go through that. One time they were showing us some bugs that we had supposedly dropped on them. One of our pilots just picked it up and ate it. He did a little solitary time for that."

Lee was right, I had to go through a few more sessions where they tried to get information out of me. They always ended up beating on me before I was sent back to my cell. Lee was also right when he said they would eventually give up if I wouldn't give them anything.

The days turned into weeks and the weeks turned into months. We all lost a lot of weight from not getting enough to eat. Sometimes something would get us all sick, which was mostly dysentery. The poor condition we were in combined with dysentery took several lives.

After over 10 months of being imprisoned, we were told that an agreement was made to stop the fighting and we would be part of an exchange of prisoners. We suddenly started to receive more and better food. We were constantly reminded that our captors had treated us well. They tried to get some to sign a statement that said we had been well treated. I don't know of anyone who did sign it.

The exchange was slow in coming and progressed at a slow pace. We all, both sides, had to pass over a bridge in a demilitarized zone that later came to be known as the Freedom Bridge.

We were taken to one of our bases in Japan, interrogated to great lengths and given a complete physical. Our loved ones had been notified as soon as they could be, and we were allowed to make a phone call to them after that. I had been listed as killed in action, so this was the best way to handle the notification. If not, the shock of my voice may have given my parents a heart attack. My mother answered the phone and started crying so hard she couldn't talk and had to pass the phone to my Dad. She was able later to get back on. It was a day one can never forget.

During my physical, it was discovered that the beatings I had received injured my left shoulder. They would look at it closer, but the doctor did not think I would regain full use of it again. That, of course, meant I would not be able to fly.

This was very difficult for me to accept. I wanted to stay in the Navy and make it my career. If I could not fly, I didn't think I would be able to. I had to fly, that was a given, and if I couldn't fly in the Navy, I would find another way. I am sure the doctor understood how I felt. He promised me he would look at every possibility to find a way to repair it.

After arriving back in the United States, we were given leave so we could go home. I had learned in Japan that I had been listed as being killed in action. I was able to get in contact with our Skipper by phone. I think he dropped the phone when I told him who I was. He told me that Jake had seen me engage the first Mig and shoot it down, followed by the other Mig shooting me down. He had gotten behind the last Mig and did a lot of damage to him right after he had gotten me. He reported that I was trailing heavy smoke and entered a spin at close to 30,000 feet, he tried to follow me down, but I was spinning so hard he couldn't stay with me. He went down to 10,000 feet and lost me for a short time. He never saw a chute, but he saw where the plane crashed into the ground. He reported that I had to have been in the plane when it crashed. They were so sure an attempt to find me never took place. I told him Lee was alive also. We agreed to get together as soon as we could so he could bring me up to date on all that had happened.

I was literally beside myself to see Danny. I thought I would like to knock on her door and surprise her. I was a little hesitant, thinking It might be too great a shock, but I decided to do it anyway. Then I repented and decided to call if I could find where she was.

It wasn't easy, but I finally found that she was at an Army base in Georgia. It took almost two hours to track her down. She was on duty, doing the patient rounds with a doctor. I finally got to the phone on the floor she was on and talked to that desk. They told me they would find her if I would hold. I readily agreed.

It was several minutes before I heard a soft voice say hello. I asked if she was setting down. She said no. I asked her to sit down. I think she recognized my voice, but I was supposed to be dead. "Are you sitting down now?"

A weak reply came back with a "Yes."

"Danny, this is Max, I am not dead, I am alive." All I could hear was silence until the phone hit the floor. That was unmistakable. I heard a lot of noises like people shuffling around. I was yelling into the phone, but no one would pick it up. Finally, I heard someone say hello. "What happened? Did Danny faint?"

All I heard was, "Who is this?"

"I'm a friend of Danny's. I was reported dead when I was shot down, but I didn't die. How is Danny?"

"Just a minute, I think she can talk now."

All I heard was, "Max, you're dead."

"I'm not dead, Danny, I was able to eject from my plane before it crashed. I was taken prisoner by the North Koreans and just released a few days ago. I should have called you before while I was in Japan, but I wanted to tell you in person. After I decided that may be too much of a shock, I decided to call from home. Is everything going Alright for you?"

There was a silence followed by. "Max, I thought you were dead."

"I know, Danny, you just told me that."

Slowly Danny came back hesitating and taking deep breaths. "It has been almost a year. I was sure you were dead and had given up all hope. I knew you were dead. Why didn't you let me know?"

"Danny, you're not rational, you know I couldn't let you know. Is something wrong? Is there something I need to know?"

Another long hesitation, "Max, I started dating someone else. I didn't know, Max, I didn't know you were alive."

I had a feeling as though I had just been run over by a Mac truck. I couldn't speak; I couldn't even think straight. I was searching for words but couldn't find them. "I understand Danny, let's just say it's the luck of the draw. I had no way of telling you I was alive, and you had no way of knowing I was alive. I think I understand, but I'm not even sure of that. Right now perhaps it would have been better for both of us if I was dead.

I just now did receive a death sentence, not to my life, only to my dreams. I wish you the best, Danny, and all the happiness that life can give. If you are ever in the neighborhood, look me up. Goodbye." With that, I simply let go of the phone and let it drop. I could hear Danny's voice as I walked away.

I walked over to a cabinet and poured myself a stiff shot of Jim Beam whiskey and threw it down. Just then, my mother walked in. It wasn't difficult for her to see something was definitely not right. She looked at me and heard Danny still on the phone, so she walked over to it and said hello. She mostly listened for a while and simply said, "OK." My mother looked at me and said, "Someone wants to talk to you."

"Not now, Mom."

"Max, get over here and talk to this girl."

"I can't, Mom."

"Yes, you can, and you will."

I walked over to the phone and simply said, "Hello." Danny was crying so hard she could hardly talk. I simply said. "I understand, Danny, forgive me for my rudeness. It was nobody's fault. It was just something that happened. I don't think any less of you. You must know how disappointed I am. You just didn't know, and I couldn't tell you. I do sincerely wish you happiness."

"Max, I can't go through with this, he has asked me to marry him. I need time to think."

"Don't do that, Danny, I can't see that proving anything. Live your life, and I'll find a way to live mine. Our lives touched for a fleeting moment, and for a while, we shared a dream. Dreams are really only wishes, and this wish didn't come true for me. You have a new dream to live, live it to its fullest."

Danny wanted the phone number here at my parents and insisted I take hers. She asked me to promise her I would call before I made any big decisions in my life.

Of course, my Mom wanted to know all about Danny, so I explained to her what had happened. I told her I had decided to leave the Navy since I was sure they would not allow me to fly again. Mom asked me what I would do and where I would go. I just explained that I had no plans but would like to get back into flying. She said I could stay with them as long as I like. I thanked her and told her she was a great Mom.

I had learned that my old squadron was still together and now at Alameda in Oakland, California. Since the war had ended, there was not a need to form new squadrons until they had made the readjustment to a peacetime Navy. VF–21 had lost a couple more pilots, but the fighting for them had not been as severe after we took out the bridges. I was also told I would not be allowed to return to a fighter squadron. In fact, I was now grounded until a decision was made on my ability to fly. I was told that it did not look good.

I was disappointed, of course, and told the skipper I would like to request a termination of my active duty. The skipper said he understood completely and would give it his approval. In the meantime, our squadron had exchanged its F9F-5 Panther jets for the new F9F-6 Cougar. The Cougar had swept wings and was capable of breaking the sound barrier.

Even with all the disappointment I just had, it was great to get back with the squadron and see my old friends again. Jake had advanced to a flight leader, and some of my young Ensigns had become section leaders. They had a good squadron record and had received a commendation. It was very difficult to see them flying and me just sitting on the ground. There was a T-33 jet trainer available with two seats. I think sometimes there was an argument as to who would take me up to get my flight time. I know they were some of the finest men I had ever met or even hoped to meet.

Now all I had to do was wait for my release from active duty and try to figure out what I would do after I did receive it.

My Mom had forwarded some notes from Danny. They said how sorry she was and that she would like to talk to me. Some were addressed to Mom, where Danny told her how much she would like to meet her and my Dad.

It was tough for me just sitting around watching the other guys flying the new Cougar. Every time I looked at it, I kept telling myself this was just a dream and it would end soon.

Each day became more boring and even more disappointing than the day before. I wanted to get out of the Navy, but I had no idea what I would do until one morning when I walked into the squadron area. A sailor approached me and told me the Skipper wanted to see me.

I assumed my discharge papers had arrived, and I would be cast adrift into the sea of life. I would have to learn how to survive in a different world, one I was unaccustomed to and did not want. A world that could devour and spit me out in little pieces. I walked down to the Skipper's office. I didn't hurry, I kind of strolled, not sure I wanted to accept the inevitable I knew was about to happen. I reached up, hesitated, and knocked on the Skipper's door. I heard the Skipper say, "Come in."

As I entered the room, the Skipper stood up and was joined by a French officer who also stood up. The French officer held the rank of Colonel. I was completely puzzled. The Skipper introduced me to the Colonel, who was Colonel Ambert. The Colonel stepped forward and grabbed my hand in a firm handshake.

The Skipper began, "Have a seat, Max, we may have something here you may be interested in. Colonel Ambert is with the French Foreign Legion. They are currently in a conflict in Vietnam. They have purchased twelve F8F Bearcat world war two fighters from us. As you know, the F8F is not a tame bird and has many characteristics that are different from other planes. They need someone who has flown the F8F to help their pilots learn how to fly them. Your records show that you have about forty hours in the F8F. Is that true?"

"Yes, sir, it is. I flew both the Hellcat and Bearcat. Believe me, the Bearcat is an awesome plane and not easy for pilots to tame. I lost a couple of friends in them."

"Here is the deal, Max, our Navy will keep you on their payroll for an undetermined amount of time if you help deliver them to the Legion. Nothing is said about flying. They will turn their head the other way so you can do whatever you must do to train the Legion pilots. The Legion has also agreed to pay you a Capitaine's (equal to a Navy senior Lieutenant) salary and flight pay while you are with them. You, as a US Navy pilot, cannot fly in combat with the Legion and that is one thing they will enforce. I would advise you not to step over that line unless you want to get canned. Is that something you would be interested in?"

"I would like to ask the Colonel if my not knowing French will be a deterrent?"

The Colonel, after a brief chuckle, said that some of the pilots can't either, but all could speak English.

I looked at the Colonel, smiled, and said, "When do I start?"

The Colonel smiled back, "You just did. I will give you a quick briefing now, and we can get together tomorrow. I will give you more rules and information you will need at that time. You will also need to see the Admiral here; they will want to finalize everything.

It is important that you wear a US Navy uniform and be classified as an advisor to the Legion. You will be living in the Officers' Quarters and have full privileges of a Legion officer. You will be transported to France from the US by your Navy. The training of our pilots will take place in France and later continue in Vietnam. For the last phase, we would like to have you go to Vietnam and help set up the F8F squadron there. You will be paid for six months of service, if we accomplish our goal ahead of six months, we will release you early, but you will still receive six months' pay. If the setup and training of the F8F squadron are considered successful, you will receive a $5,000.00 bonus for each month you spend with the Legion. If you choose to leave early or the setup is not considered successful, this bonus will be forfeited. Oh yes, if you would care to learn French, we will provide you with a tutor at our expense. It would be to our advantage for you to speak French, but it will not be a problem if you do not speak our language. Any questions so far?"

"You've covered a lot of ground, Colonel. Let me digest that now, and I will make a list if I have any more questions. When would you like to meet tomorrow?"

"You may want to stop at the Admiral's office first, so why don't we get together for lunch and continue our meeting in the afternoon?"

"We can meet at the Officers Club for lunch and then use one of the squadron rooms to talk," I replied.

The Colonel offered me a handshake. "I can be at the Officers Club at noon, will that work for you?"

I extended my hand, "I'll see you then."

I visited the Admirals office the next morning and received my orders and was briefed on what was expected of me. I started to feel like a spy being sent on an espionage mission in some dark corner of the world. I would not be allowed to go to Vietnam with the Legion squadron without approval from the Admiral. They felt it would be alright, but the permission was necessary. I had a pleasant surprise when I was told the Admiral felt I should be advanced to the rank of Lieutenant Commander. This would give me more authority, and I would have a higher rank than most of the Legion pilots. This point was simple to understand. I was also told that they would inform the Legion so they could adjust their pay schedule to that of a Legion Commandant. I was given five days to get ready.

I met with the Colonel for lunch. He had been informed about the change in rank and was in full agreement with it. We had a pleasant time together, going over anything about my new assignment that we felt necessary. The Colonel departed the next day for France, I followed in five days.

CHAPTER VIII

I had been warned not to disclose any of the details with anybody. This was considered a classified mission. As such, it could not be disclosed or discussed at all. I knew I would have to tell my parents that I would be out of the country for several months, and I could only be reached personally in an emergency. They would have a phone number they could call to an office that would determine if the reason was valid. Mail could flow through the Fleet Post Office, but it would be censored.

I would be able to call before the time I left with a brief explanation that I would not be able to discuss my work because it was classified. It was apparent that this assignment was indeed a clandestine mission. I gave my family reassurance that I would be alright, and the government was just overreacting to some classified material I may have to handle. When I called, Mom answered the phone. We had a pleasant conversation about how everyone was doing and small talk about the weather and such things. I told her I would be on an assignment that would not give me much time for writing, and the phone service would not be readily available. I think she sensed that I was not giving her all the information I had, but she accepted my explanation without question.

She told me that Danny had called and talked to her. She also said that she thought Danny was a very nice girl. She hoped to meet her someday. Danny wanted my address; which Mom gave her. Mom also told Danny that she would make sure I answered her. She gave me Danny's address, since I would be difficult to write to and insisted that I write to Danny first. I reluctantly promised Mom I would. I was not able to talk to Dad since he was not home. It was a pleasant conversation that ended well.

I knew I would have to write to Danny, so I decide to do it right then. Might as well get it done. I grabbed a pen and paper and sat down.

"Dear Danny, I must apologize for the way I acted when I talked to you the other day. I just didn't expect that you would be dating that soon. I do remember the short time it took me to get to like you. I am not blaming you for anything, it was just something neither of us could control.

I can't change the way I feel about you, but I am very disappointed you could forget me so soon. I know you thought I was dead. You had every right to do what you did. I wouldn't have much to offer you now, which would be difficult for me to deal with.

I have an assignment ahead of me, but I do plan on leaving the Navy soon after. I have been told I would not be able to fly again after the injury I received at the hands of the North Koreans. That is very difficult for me to accept. I will have to make major changes in my life to adjust to a new life I will have to live. I sincerely do feel it will be a problem for me. I am afraid I may let it show. I don't think you would want to be around an old grouch. I think it would have been better if I had not called. I am sure it would have saved us both a lot of grief.

Danny, perhaps you will allow me to write to you occasionally. If you don't want to answer, it is certainly not necessary and alright with me. I will have very limited ability to call or receive any calls for some time.

By the way, my Mom thinks you are wonderful. Don't be surprised if you hear from her in the future. I know the two of you would have been close friends.

I do wish you the best, Danny. Perhaps it is time to close the book. Maybe it was just a chapter about the time we knew each other. I am sure you have chosen a great guy to spend your time with." I just signed my name.

The next few days were spent getting ready to go to France. I had to have my new rank changed on my uniforms. I also had new name patches put on my flight suits with LCDR Max Bradley on them. If I have the opportunity to fly, you can bet I will take it. I had been told the Navy would look the other way while I was with the Legion. I fully intended to take advantage of any such opportunity. It would be necessary for me to take my flight gear, such as my helmet, with me. I was not to wear anything that suggested I was a Legion officer. I was an adviser from the US Navy and had to look like one.

The day before I left for France, I reported to the Admiral's office for a final briefing. It was mostly a review of what I had been told before. Everything was still in place. It was, however, emphasized that I was always to be aware of the US and French relations.

The next morning, I boarded a Navy P2V patrol plane and was on my way to France. We would make a couple of stops, but it would be a direct flight.

We were flying east losing time, so it was late in the afternoon when we did arrive at the French military airfield in Istres. Istres is about 90 KM east of Aubagne, the French headquarters of the Legion in France. I was welcomed to the Legion headquarters by my friend Colonel Ambert. Some introductions followed, including the commanding officer of the new F8 squadron, Commandant Roubalay. I met a couple of the Legion pilots as well.

It was getting late, so I needed to find my temporary quarters. I would be at Aubagne for the initial part of my stay and would move to Istres when the planes arrived. We would set up our headquarters there and do all our training from Istres. Commandant Roubalay agreed to meet me for dinner later. He would call for me at 1900. As he dropped me off at the Officers' Quarters, he asked if I would mind if he brought a couple friends along. I, of course, said I would like to meet some more of his friends and that they would be very welcome.

I departed, went into the building, and found my room. My gear had arrived and was already there. I did not go to any extent to organize the room since I knew I would be there only for a brief time. I decided to get a shower and rest a little before my new friend, John Roubalay, returned to pick me up. The time passed rather quickly. John was here before I realized it. He had parked his car outside and had come into the building to get me. We greeted each other with a handshake and the proper salutation. I asked if he had brought his friends along. He replied that he had, they were in his car waiting for us.

"I won't keep your friends waiting. I am anxious to meet them. Are they some of the pilots that will be flying with us?"

"No, they are just some personal friends that I would like you to meet." He replied.

We walked out to his car, which was a fancy sports car. As we approached the car, the doors opened, and two very attractive ladies stepped out. I was surprised and stopped abruptly.

John promptly introduced me to the ladies. One was introduced as Adele, the other as Sarah. He explained that Adele was the girl he had been dating for some time. Sarah was her close friend who happened to be at Adele's. Adele had asked John to let her come along because Sarah was going to stay overnight at Adele's, and she didn't want to leave her home alone.

John said, "I should have said something, but I didn't think you would mind. I hope you don't."

"John, I can't think of a reason why I should. I will admit that it has been some time since I have had the pleasure of having such a lovely lady as a companion. Perhaps I should ask Sarah if she objects having me as her escort. I hope being her escort is the proper word. I don't want to be presumptuous. Sarah, am I wording that correctly?"

Sarah smiled. "After meeting you, I think I would prefer to call it a date."

I smiled back. "A date it is then. I think I feel a little more comfortable with that also."

Sarah smiled again and said. "I don't believe you are telling the truth when you said it has been some time since you have had a date. I hope you are not married."

"No, I am not married. I just happen to have had an unrequested stay in North Korea for about a year."

John jerked his head around and looked at me. "Were you a prisoner?"

"I was shot down and spent almost a year in one of North Korea's prisons. I was released when the war ended."

"Max, I would like to hear about that sometime."

"Maybe we can swap a few stories. I am sure you have had some interesting times in the Legion to tell me about."

The evening proved to be very pleasant. We enjoyed a lovely dinner and even danced a bit. Sarah was a delightful person. She had a charming personality as well as being intelligent. I immediately liked her, but I knew I was not ready for a serious relationship. Danny was still planted firmly in my mind. Even though she was seeing someone else, I couldn't stop thinking about her. I would have to get over Danny before someone new entered my life.

John and I decided we would meet for breakfast so he could tell me more about the new Legion squadron. We would get together with the rest of the pilots at 0900 here at Legion headquarters. This was Tuesday, and the new planes would come in the following Monday. That would give us the rest of the week for me to explain some of the features and characteristics of the F8. I had brought along some handbooks. Some of the people who would work on the planes had been in the US to go through schooling there. They would come in with the planes that were on the aircraft carrier Hornet. That would give them more time to familiarize themselves with the F8. The planes would be offloaded and taken directly to Istres.

All the pilots and I would be stationed at Istres from that time on until the squadron moved to Vietnam.

The indoctrination of the Legion pilots went well. I had fifteen pilots, including John. I found out why the Legion was called the Foreign Legion. Seven different nationalities were represented among the fifteen pilots. By the end of the week, I felt comfortable with the progress we had made. We would be ready for a hands-on training period before they actually flew the F8.

John told me that Sarah would like to see me again and that he and Adele had a date that evening. He wondered if I would care to go along with Sarah as my date. He could call Adele and have her call Sarah.

I thanked him and said. "I think I would enjoy seeing Sarah again and I do need to relax a bit. I believe it would be more personal if I called Sarah and asked her myself. Would Adele mind?"

"Not at all, that would be a good idea. I am sure it will earn you some points. I've never had the opportunity to tell you about Sarah, have I?"

"No, you haven't. Is there something I should know about Sarah?"

"You should know who she is and a little about her background. She doesn't date a lot, so you should consider yourself very fortunate. I am sure you have not seen many French movies if you don't know about Sarah."

"You have certainly gotten my attention, and I know nothing about Sarah."

"Max, I think I have said too much. I will let Sarah tell you what she wants you to know. Ask her later about her work. If she wants you to know, she will tell you."

"John, you are a very mysterious man. Will you give me Sarah's number, or do I have to guess what that is also?"

John smiled, wrote something on a piece of paper, and handed it to me. I accepted it and started for my room. I dialed the number on the paper when I arrived at my room. I heard someone say hello in French, or at least I thought it was French. I asked to speak to Sarah. There was an abrupt change, I heard, "Is that you, Max?"

"Yes It is, am I speaking to Sarah?

"Yes, you are."

"Sarah, I was going to call to ask if you would care to have dinner and spend a little time together this evening. John and Adele were going out and asked if we would like to accompany them. John asked me if I knew who you were. Is there something I should know? Are you some mysterious person that preys on unsuspecting American Sailors?"

"If that were true, it would be only the ones I like. If the invitation is still open, I would like very much to accept, or have you changed your mind?"

"No, not at all. I am very pleased that you have accepted. I will talk to John and see what their plans are. I am kind of tied to what they are planning. Will that work for you?"

"Actually, I would like to get to know you better. Would you mind if I picked you up, so we can have more time to talk? Just the two of us."

"Sarah, I think it would be nice. No, I know I would like that. In fact, I would love to spend some time alone with you. I would really like to get to know you better also. I am still wondering what John was trying to tell me."

"I am open to all questions. May I pick you up at seven?"

"Sarah, seven will work fine for me if I must wait that long."

"I will be there promptly at seven, see you then."

As I hung up the phone, I was wondering who this mystery woman was that I was about to date. I realized I didn't have a clue. I could only wait and see. I grabbed a shower and dressed. It occurred to me that I may not be dressed for anything formal, but I had my uniform on which should qualify either way. The way Sarah talked, we would just spend the evening with John and Adele then leisurely talking to one another later alone. Either way, she will have to accept me as I am. I made myself a martini, put on a record of the Swan Lake opera, and settled in to relax until she arrived. The music was almost hypnotic as it progressed into the Dance of The Swans. A blanket of sorts seemed to descend and cover me with a feeling of warmth and comfort. It was like I was floating in a dream, a dream I really did not want to escape from. I wanted to stay there forever and cast the troubled world behind me. I was jarred back to reality when I heard a horn sound off.

I hurriedly turned off the music and started for the door. As I reached for the door handle, it opened suddenly, and Sarah stepped into the room. "Max, I couldn't wait for another minute to see you. I don't want to be mysterious; I want you to like me." I did not have a second to respond. She threw her arms around me and pleaded. "Please like me."

It rather startled me and made me jerk back a little. Sarah released me and stepped back. "Did I scare you, Max, or wasn't I supposed to do that?"

"Sarah, I just wasn't ready, it did surprise me. Can we start over? I promise I'll be ready this time."

Sarah smiled, stepped toward me, put her arms around my neck, and gave me one of the most passionate kisses I have ever had. She looked up at me with a glowing smile and said, "Was that better?"

I seemed to be able only to nod my head in agreement, but finally said, "Yes."

Sarah smiled again and said, "I know a secluded little place where we can dine and enjoy a glass of wine while we talk. Will that be OK?"

"Sounds wonderful to me, in fact, if you are there any place would be wonderful. I thought we were to meet John and Adele."

"Adele called and said that John had something come up, so they postponed their date until tomorrow night. I didn't tell you because, this way, I can see you twice. Do you mind?"

"Of course not."

We walked out arm in arm to her car. I helped her in and noticed it was a Porsche sports car. As I recall, they are very expensive. I just commented on what a nice car she had.

"I am glad you like it, maybe you would like to drive it sometime."

"Maybe later, for now, I would rather just be able to look at the beautiful girl driving it."

"Thank you, that was very sweet of you."

We finally arrived at a small café in a rather quiet area. As we went in, we were greeted by the owner who treated Sarah like she was of royal lineage. The owner spoke to Sarah in French as he pointed to a table in a rather darkened corner. Sarah replied in English, telling him I did not speak French, and would he please use English.

He smiled and shook his head in agreement. "Of course." He turned to me and continued. "Miss Bouquet prefers that table. I think she likes it because people will be less likely to notice her in the dim light. Is that right, Miss Bouquet?"

Sarah just chuckled a bit and said. "You know me too well, Pierre."

After we were seated, I couldn't help but ask. "You must come here often, are you hiding from someone?"

Sarah simply replied, "Sort of."

I looked inquisitively at Sarah and said. "Sarah, you have my complete and full attention, I hope you will explain a few things to me."

"May I order a glass of wine first?"

I nodded. "Certainly."

After the wine arrived, Sarah began. "Max, John reminded me you were a prisoner in Korea for a long time. I am sorry that happened to you. That and the fact that you probably don't see a lot of French movies would be reason enough for you not to have heard of me. I don't want to appear to be egotistical when I tell you I have been successful in movies and have also appeared in some of your American films. You have been out of touch with the world for a long time, and I am sure you never saw me in a movie." Sarah just looked at me. I knew she was waiting for me to say something.

"That sounds wonderful, Sarah, why were you so afraid to tell me this?"

Sarah hesitated, looked down at the table. When she looked up, she looked straight into my eyes. "The first time I saw you, I liked you. I wanted you to like me, but not for the wrong reason. I wanted you to like me as the person I am and not because I had been in some movies. If that was wrong of me, please forgive me. I still want you to like me, Max. My past experiences with men have not been good. I want to change that, Max. I want someone to like me, and even love me for the person I am. Is that too much to ask?"

"No, Sarah, it's not too much to ask at all. I must admire you for the way you feel. I can't blame you for hiding this from me. If you truly feel the way you say you do, it was the perfect way to handle the situation. I could never be angry with you. I can only tell you again that I admire you for the way you feel. Perhaps someday you will have to choose between the two ways of life. The one of fame will be hard to discard. Have you been married before?"

"I don't like to tell you this, but I have been married twice."

"Sarah, I would like to tell you a little about me, do you mind?"

"I want to hear about you, Max."

"I am not sure I know where to start. My life is flying, a life like that is not conducive to a happy marriage. I have been in my share of combat and brushes with death. I am not sure I could ask a wife to live a life like that. The Navy has said it will not let me fly anymore because of the injuries I received from beatings in a Korean prison camp. I will find another way, and I have now with the Legion. This will end, but I will again find another way.

There is also a girl in my life. I met her when she took care of me in an Army Field Hospital after I was shot down the first time. I didn't know her for a very long time, but I did fall in love with her. When I was shot down the second time, I was reported as killed in action. I then spent the better part of a year in a Korean prison camp.

I never saw her after I came home, but I did talk to her on the phone. She was seeing someone else. She told me she was not sure she wanted to continue her relationship with this other man, but I did not encourage her to end it.

Sarah, I have no idea where my feelings are and what I should do. I don't want to mislead you, but I will admit that I like you. I'll be very busy with the Legion, and I plan on going to Vietnam with them. Anything can happen. We both have a lot to consider. Can you accept being friends for now? I'm not sure I will even live through this, and that is not fair to you. Can we be friends?"

"Do I have a choice, Max?"

"Yes, you could say goodbye and just walk away from me."

"I don't want to do that, Max. Is that what you want me to do?"

"Sarah, I think you know I don't want that. I don't want to be your plaything and thrown away when you get tired of me either."

"Is that what you think, Max?"

"I'm not sure what to think. That is why I suggested we settle for friendship and see where it will lead us. Do you have a problem for us to spend some time together and get to know each other? That should be the way any relationship should start."

"Maybe you are right. If that is the only way I can hold on to you, I will take it."

And so, our relationship continued. You might say on a trial basis. I knew I had a responsibility to the Legion, and I did intend to honor that responsibility to the best of my ability. I wanted to see every one of my Legion pilots come back alive and that was what I was going to do if possible.

CHAPTER IX

Over the weekend I moved my gear to the airfield at Istres and joined the rest of the pilots who would be flying the F8. Sunday John and I took Adele and Sarah to an early dinner so we would be sharp when the planes came in on Monday. We had a nice time. Sarah was very conservative in her behavior, which made me wonder what she was thinking. As we parted, Sarah gave me a very warm hug and passionate kiss. She whispered in my ear so John and Adele would not hear. "How am I doing, Max? I was almost going to say I love you, but I will just say I like you, so you don't run away."

I returned. "That's not fair, Sarah, you give me a kiss like that, brush me off, and just walk away."

"I can do better if you want me to."

I smiled and really planted a kiss on her. "That will do just fine, for now, thank you." We both laughed and shared a very warm hug.

The next morning all the Legion pilots showed up in our ready room. John told me that the Hornet, with our planes, would not be in for several hours. He told me he had never been on an aircraft carrier and wondered if the Commanding Officer of the Hornet would mind if we would fly out to it in a chopper and come in with them.

"I really don't see why not. Can I get a dispatch out to him asking if he would allow the two of us to do that?"

"You write it up, and I'll get it sent," John replied.

I wrote a short request and gave it to John, knowing that he would take care of it.

In a short time, we received a dispatch back from the Skipper of the Hornet saying that we were quite welcome to come aboard. John already had a chopper waiting. I told John that I would be more comfortable in my flight suit flying out to the ship, so we both changed, grabbed our helmets and May West, and headed for the chopper. The ride out to the ship only took about 30 minutes. As we settled onto the deck, the Skipper of the Hornet was there to meet us. We both saluted him as we stepped out of the chopper and shook hands. He welcomed us aboard, and after a short conversation turned us over to the executive officer. The executive officer told us that we would be in port in about three hours and asked if we would like to see our new planes. We both answered in unison with a yes. We made our way to the hangar deck where all twelve of our planes were stored. I think they looked beautiful to both John and me.

In the conversation that followed, we were asked if we would like to fly a couple back. I looked at John, and he looked at me. I knew he wanted to. The look in his eyes was unmistakable.

I was the first to break the silence. "John, you have never flown the F8, I am not sure that would be a good idea."

"I am sure I can handle it, and I have never flown off an aircraft carrier."

"It would be different, John if you had flown the F8 before, but you have not. This isn't your usual bird, believe me. I'm not as worried about the takeoff as I am the landing."

"Don't make me pull rank on you, Max."

"I'm against it, but it's your funeral. If something goes wrong, I'm the one who will have to answer all the questions. I can about guarantee you that you will not be here to answer any. Still want to do it?"

"You bet I do."

I looked at the executive officer and said, "Is that OK with you, Commander?"

The Commander shrugged his shoulders and said. "I don't have any jurisdiction; he is not in my Navy."

I turned to the Commander and said. "Give me some time to go over a few things with this hardheaded Legionnaire. I think he knows the cockpit, but I'll try to give him a few tips."

"You got it, let me know when you're ready. I'll get a couple planes up on the flight deck and have them ready. Give me a little warning so we can turn into the wind. I assume you will want to just make a deck run on your takeoff."

"I've got enough trouble, don't put him on a catapult."

John and I picked an airplane and started going over the basics and what he could expect. I will admit he had everything down. He must have been doing his homework.

When I felt he was ready, we ventured up to the flight deck and asked that the ship be turned into the wind. I made sure John had his plane started, and everything was set where it should be. I then got in my plane, started it, and notified control we were ready when they were. By this time, the launch officer was on the deck between the two of us. He received a signal that the ship was ready, so he looked at John and gave him a thumbs up which was asking if he was ready. John returned the thumbs up. The Launch officer gave John a turning motion with his hand and waited. John went to full power and saluted the launch officer, which was his signal he was ready to be launched. The launch officer dropped his arm and pointed down the deck, telling John to go. John literally jumped into the air and was on his way. I was next and went through the same procedure. As we climbed out, I caught John and joined up on him in formation. We headed for Istres, which would only take less than twenty minutes.

I pulled in pretty tight on John and gave him a thumbs up telling him he did OK. John called the tower and requested landing instructions. At first, the tower wasn't sure who we were until John explained. To my surprise, John requested a low high-speed pass before we landed.

I just shook my head so he could see me. The high-speed pass was granted, so we went by the tower at about 300 knots. As we were in our pass, John asked me to slip back a little. It wasn't too hard to tell what he was about to do. I watched as he did two slow rolls in succession as he pulled up. Not to be outdone, I followed suit. I joined up on him again as he turned to make our break over the runway to land. The landings went well, and I breathed a sigh of relief as we were taxiing. When we came to a stop, I noticed that all the other pilots were out to greet us. I am sure John had a smile from ear to ear as he climbed out of the plane. I was just enjoying the fact that John had done so well, and he was in one piece.

The enthusiasm and excitement among the pilots were running rampant. It appeared they all wanted to get in the cockpit at the same time. John was being besieged with questions of how did it fly and every other imaginal thing they could think of to ask. John was wearing a smile from ear to ear and gesturing with his hands how it turned and so forth. I was very pleased with the reception. I knew we had to get busy the next day and get our groundwork done, so the rest of the pilots could get into the air.

It took the Hornet several more hours before it came in and docked. The offloading and transporting of the planes to the field went on into the early evening. The Commander of the Legion base had invited the Captain and Executive officer of the Hornet to dinner. He also included John and me. I had only met the Legion Commanding Officer once, so it did give me a chance to get a little more acquainted. It was a very cordial dinner and enjoyed by all who were there. I said my goodbyes to the Hornet Captain and Executive Officer after dinner since they would be leaving early in the morning. I knew the next day would be a busy day, and so did John, so we called it an early evening and went to our quarters.

The bugler woke me when he announced revelry the next morning with the piercing sound of his bugle that shattered the stillness and called the entire world to attention. I thought anyone who could sleep through that just couldn't be human. I dressed and made my way to the officer's mess. I am not sure what they called it there, but it was still the mess to me. Many of the pilots were already there, and John came in a little later. The talk, of course, was centered around the new planes. John and I had set up the schedule we would follow.

We had already covered the cockpit and instruments. Now we would concentrate on the handling characteristics and get the feel of the plane on the ground. I would start them out on starting the engine and ground control followed by short aborted takeoff runs. They would have to be cautious on the aborted takeoff, so they didn't get into the air. The F8 was so quick that it could easily be done. It did happen with another student when I was in advanced training. The day ended with a promise that they would fly the F8 tomorrow. I would break them up in pairs so that two of them could work together. We would get as many as we could into the air tomorrow and follow with the rest the following day.

We had a good day, which was followed by more good days as we progressed with our training. We spent several weeks progressing from one stage to the next until I felt we were ready for the task at hand. This had covered two and a half months, making it three months since I had been assigned to the Legion. In the last few weeks, John and I did not spend a lot of time with Adele and Sarah. We were just too busy.

I had been receiving frequent letters from my mother, giving me news about the family and that Danny had been in contact with her. She had become fond of Danny. In her last letter, she told me that she had talked to Danny on the phone and that Danny asked if she could come and meet her. Mom asked me if I would mind if she did allow Danny to come for a visit.

I had not had time to answer Mom, and that had been over a week ago. I wanted to call her, but I had been asked not to make phone calls since it would give away my location. I thought it wouldn't take much for anyone to find me anyway, but I would play their game.

Mom said that Danny would like to hear from me. She hadn't given her my address since I had asked her not to give it to her. So, Mom sent Danny's and asked me to please write to her because Danny really wanted to know about me.

The next day was a Sunday, and we were taking the day off, so I thought maybe that would be a good day to write to Mom and consider writing to Danny. I had a brief mental argument with myself about why I should write to Danny.

She had done nothing out of the way. If she thought I was dead, it would be only fitting to give her attention to someone else. She had her life to live, and she should capture any happiness she could. I'm not sure what I was thinking. Maybe I was just hurt because I thought she should not have forgotten me so soon. It really wasn't soon at all. I had been declared dead for some months, so she had no reason to believe otherwise.

On the flip side, it had taken three or four months to declare me dead, so I would have thought she would have waited sometime after that. I just could not validate a reason in my mind to justify what she did, and I did not want to interfere with her plans with another man. I thought that it all came down to the fact that I was just plain jealous and acted like some juvenile. I made up my mind to write to both Mom and Danny on Sunday.

John had walked up behind me and startled me when he took hold of my shoulder. John said that he and Adele would be going out to dinner and maybe find a place to dance afterward. He wanted to know if I would like to get a date with Sarah and come along. I just told him I would call Sarah and see if she was busy.

I did go to the phone and made a call to Sarah. I was surprised when Sarah answered in English. I wondered if I was set up for this and Sarah was expecting me to call, so she answered in English instead of French. She agreed to go with me and said she would like to pick me up so we could have some time together afterward.

I agreed, so she offered to pick me up at seven. She said she knew where John and Adele would go, and we could just meet them there. I told her that would be fine, but I wondered how she knew where they would go. We had gone to so many places. I guess it really didn't matter. However, I was sure she had talked to Adele.

I found John in his office. "John, Sarah said she would pick me up at seven, and we would meet you at where we would dine. Somehow, she said she knew where you would be. I think she must have talked to Adele."

"I wouldn't doubt that, Max, those two girls are always hatching something up."

I replied. "Sarah told me she wanted to spend some time with me afterward. Maybe I should just take that as a compliment and be happy."

John looked a little puzzled. "I do know she likes you a lot and can't figure out why you aren't more receptive to her. Adele tells me a lot of things about Sarah. She has told Adele that you treat her differently than most men.

Sarah has always had men falling at her feet and doing everything she wants them to do, I mean like she calls all the plays, and the men follow along like little puppy dogs on a leash. She said that you treat her differently. I think that has surprised her and she can't figure you out."

"John, sometimes I feel like I am just another conquest for her, and she wants to conquer me and declare who the victor is and move on to the next challenge."

"Max, don't tell Adele I said anything, but I like you, and I want to keep you as a friend. I like Sarah too, but I know she must be the dominant figure in everything she does. That doesn't mean you can't change her. If anyone can, you can."

"We have a lot ahead of us, John. I'm not ready to make any commitments to anyone until we finish our work. I am going to Vietnam with you, and I won't take no for an answer. You and the rest of the pilots are a part of my life now, and whatever job we have in front of us, I will be a part of.

You are in command. I promise you I'll never contest that. I will also give my allegiance to you and the Legion. John, I feel that I am now a Legionnaire, and I will not disgrace the Legion in any way. I am serving with one of the finest group of men I have ever had the pleasure of serving with.

I'm not supposed to be involved in combat, but I will tell you this, if you need my help, I will be dishonored if you don't call upon me for that help. Where we are going, and what we will do will not be without cost. Men will die, and others will be maimed. I know there is not one coward in the pilots we have. I am asking you not to let me be that one coward."

"Max, what you have been through, no one could ever call you a coward. I am honored to have you with our squadron and even more honored to call you my friend. I appreciate your dedication and willingness to give me your allegiance, but whatever we do, we will do together. I may have to call the plays, but you will be with me making the decisions. If I need you and I can't figure out any other way, I will put a Legion uniform on you and declare you a Legion officer."

"Thanks, John, I think we understand each other. Right now, we have a different battle to wage. Adele and Sarah, to be specific. I'll see you wherever it is that the girls have arranged for us." With that, we both left the squadron area.

I went home, showered, and sat down to wait for Sarah. I had a little time, so I mixed a martini and sat down to enjoy some classical music. I especially enjoy the short movement called the Intermezzo when the music started low and continued to build until it resounded a high crescendo. I felt it was always inspiring and invigorating.

As it finished, I heard a knock on the door, and Sarah entered before I could answer. She came into the room, threw her arms around me, looked into my eyes. "I missed you. Don't you like me anymore?"

"You know I like you, Sarah, it's just that I don't understand you. You could have your choice of a hundred other men and yet you have befriended me. I can't understand why you would do that."

Sarah pulled herself closer to me, and passionately kissed me. "Because I like you very much, do I need another reason?"

"That depends on why you like me. Is it for another conquest you can add to your collection or do you see us growing old together?"

"I like you very much, can't we accept that and see what happens later?"

"Your right about that, Sarah. I feel the same way. I have too much ahead of me to make any firm commitments now. It does bother me that you are very famous and have been married twice. I don't want to be called number three in a list of your marriages. For now, let's just enjoy the evening and each other's company. For the records, I do enjoy your company very much, and I do like you. Will that satisfy you for now?"

"For now maybe, but I want you to do more than just like me. You can consider that a warning if you wish. I don't give up easily."

"I will consider myself forewarned."

I was happy we had that little talk. I think we both knew each other better now. We had a delightful evening. One I am sure we both would remember.

The next morning, I attended Mass and called John after to see if he wanted to have breakfast with me. John did not answer, so I was sure he had stayed over at Adele's. I knew it would be futile to call him there, so I dined alone. I thought about calling Sarah, but I felt last night went well, and it was best left the way it ended.

I decided to fulfill the promise I had made to myself and write to Mom and Danny. I wrote to Mom first. I told her

I was sorry it had taken so long for me to answer her letter and that I hoped she and Dad were in good health and feeling well. I asked her to tell my sister I loved her.

I included that I planned to write to Danny and apologize for my past behavior. I said that Danny had every right to do what she did because she thought I would not be coming home and that I hoped Danny and I could be friends. I also told Mom I was looking forward to meeting the man Danny was dating. The rest of the letter was filled with small talk. I closed with love to her and Dad.

I pondered a long time about what I would say to Danny. I finally decided just to start writing and say whatever I felt like saying. I knew there were some things I could not say, if I did, I knew they would hurt her. That was the last thing I wanted to do. I tried to tell myself that I didn't feel that strongly about Danny anymore, but I knew that wasn't true, so I just began.

"Dear Danny: Please allow me to start with an apology, that is way overdue, and I do hope you will accept it. I cannot fault you if you choose not to accept it. I was disappointed and showed it in a very juvenile way. You did nothing wrong. I am happy that you did find someone you like. I simply hope he is worthy of you.

Mom has been writing and telling me about the friendship you two have formed. I am happy for you both. Mom is a very good judge of people. I am sure you will like her, Dad, and my sister. I am not sure when I will be home again. I would like to see you again, but I am not up to it at this time. I think I have a little of that juvenile feeling still stalking me.

I am not allowed to say where I am, but I am flying again, which is my love. If I had lost that, I am sure my world would be very empty. I am with a very select group of men. One of whom has become a very close friend. I am sure it is a bond that will never be broken. I had received injuries at the hands of the North Koreans that made it questionable if I would be allowed to fly again. That has been overcome and was a big relief for me. I am happy in that respect.

Danny, I just want you to know that I am sorry for the way I acted and hope you will find it in your heart to forgive me. I still think a lot of you and hope we can continue as friends. It will no doubt always be from a distance, but nevertheless, still friends."

I just signed it with "Max."

.

CHAPTER X

It was Monday morning and the start of a new week. I arrived at our office shortly before seven. John and all the pilots were already there. Just after I arrived, Colonel Ambert walked into the room. All came to attention. Colonel Ambert walked to the front of the room and told everyone to be seated. For a moment he just looked at everybody with a very serious look. Finally, he said, "Messieurs," he stopped, looked at me, and switched to English. "Gentlemen, we will deploy in two hours.

No one is to leave the base. No phone calls and no leaving our quarters here. Twelve pilots will be assigned to fly our planes, and the rest will accompany me on a separate plane. John, you will be on the plane with me so I can brief you. Max, are you going with us or will you stay here?"

"Colonel, I'm a part of this squadron, wherever they go, I go. I do need the answer to one question."

"What is that, Max?"

"Will I be allowed to fly?"

"I didn't hear what you said, Max. I did want to mention to you, however, that you have your orders from your Navy. You'll have to follow those orders. I don't have the time to look at what you are doing. Am I to understand that you will be going with us?"

"That is affirmative, sir."

"You will accompany John and me, so I can brief you both. Thanks, Max, you have the heart of a Legionnaire. I am proud to have you with us."

"Thank you, sir."

The Colonel turned his attention back to the other pilots. "You pilots please stay here. Someone will be here briefly to give you your instructions. This is considered secret, so treat it that way. Good luck to all of you. Remember, you are a Legionnaire." The Colonel told John and me that he would brief us in John's office.

When we were in John's office, he sat down at the desk and asked us also to be seated. He began, "Gentlemen, we are going to Vietnam. We are in a bit of trouble in a place called Dien Bien Phu. Our men are completely surrounded and can only get in and out by air. We have rebuilt an old runway so we can use it to get in supplies. The fighting is fierce, and our losses have been heavy. We need to get some more air support to our men fighting there. That is why this is so urgent. We will have our pilots fly in small groups to different locations to avoid too much attention. From there, the planes will be loaded on ships and transported to Vietnam. We will be there ahead of them and fly them back in when they arrive.

Our plane is waiting for us now, and we will leave as soon as we have pilots assigned to the fighter planes. Both of you go down to where the pilots are and assign who will fly and who will lead each flight. I have three packets for you to give to the leader of each group. These are their instructions. They are to follow them to the letter with no changes whatsoever.

When you have given them their instructions, report to our plane which is in front of the hangars. We will leave as soon as you and the spare pilots get there. We have a long way to go. Any questions?"

We both offered a, "No, sir."

John and I both knew who we wanted to lead each flight. This was done quickly. We wished them all good luck and headed for our plane. We were on our way for a long ride to Vietnam. While we were in the air, we received a complete briefing from the Colonel, after which we tried to relax as much as we could.

We stopped several times to refuel and get something to eat. As spare pilots, John and I helped with the flying. It was a long flight. After we arrived in Vietnam, John and I received another complete briefing. We put together a plan we thought would work. After that, it was trying to get some rest and prepare ourselves for what we knew was ahead of us. It would be several days before our planes arrived. We had landed at Vientiane and were at that location now. Our planes would be off-loaded somewhere to the south and flown to Vientiane. The fighting was very heavy at Dien Bien Phu, so it was decided we should work from Vientiane. There were already some F8s and Corsairs' at Dien Bien Phu, and they were taking shelling from the Viet Minh.

We decided it would be better to stay in Vientiane, even though we would have to fly further to the target. It would be safer for our planes as well as the pilots and crews. We were amassing a good supply of bombs and cannon shells, and the gasoline would be much easier to obtain. The French forces were taking a lot of punishment and needed us badly. All their supplies had to be flown in or airdropped. There was absolutely no way to get them in on the ground. The only road in had been decimated, and the area was completely infiltrated with the Viet Minh. No one went in or out except by air. The French were losing, but they had to stay and fight. The casualties were immense.

Colonel Ambert would stay at Vientiane commanding that position. At least we had full control of the area around Vientiane. Finally, our planes and crews arrived. The Colonel immediately had the planes completely checked, armed, and ready for combat. They would carry two napalm bombs as well as their cannons. John was told to prepare for the first mission early the next morning. Eight would go on the mission. Whatever was left flyable would be held in reserve. We would get our target assignments that night or early in the morning. The rest of the day, we had an officer brief us on who was where and what to look for and expect. The tension was running high, but there was an eagerness among the pilots that anyone could sense. An eagerness to help their comrades who were in trouble. I couldn't help but think about the little verse that went, "There is no greater love than for one to lay down his life for a friend." John would go, but the Colonel felt it would be better for me to stay behind and keep things under control. He said he didn't want to lose me right now and have to explain it to my government. I asked him to rethink that, but he told me there would be plenty of time. He said the war is going to be there long enough for me to get involved.

He looked at me and said. "Max, you are my ace in the hole, I need you here now. I won't let both you and John go out at the same time. I am not sure I could handle this alone. To tell the truth, Max, I didn't think you would be going with us. You knew this could get ugly. You had first-hand knowledge that people get killed doing what we are doing. What motivated you?"

"Colonel, it wasn't a chance to reach some sort of a high or thrill. I had enough of that in Korea. I did want to keep flying, but the real reason is that the Legion is not fighting just to fight, they are not dying because they want to die. They are fighting for what they believe is right. They have a cause and once more a worthy cause.

They did not ask for this war, but they were not afraid to stand up for their sovereign right to live as they choose. To also defend those who would be persecuted because of their choice to live as they chose.

Under communist rule, their life would change and not for what they considered for the good. They have the right to live as they want to live, and the Legion has backed them up. Not for personal gains, but for the freedom to live as they want to live.

The Legion members would lay down their lives to defend that freedom. They are no different than the men I served with in the US Navy. Every member of the Legion, to the man, has a quality beyond explanation.

I would challenge anyone to define it or even explain it. There are no words to describe such men. They are beyond description or even understanding. The only word I can think of is "honor," and that falls far short of the commitment they have chosen.

Colonel, I am proud to be serving with the Legion, and I will not disgrace the Legion. I only ask that you accept me as another Legionnaire. I know some barriers stand in the way. When the chips are down, I ask that you treat me as you would any member of the Legion."

"Thank you, Max, from this day forward you're a member of the Legion and will be treated as a member of the Legion. You have my word on that."

There was so much tension in the air, I believe the old adage that you could cut it with a knife would apply. The eight pilots who would fly the mission had been named. The other seven would standby and be ready to go at any time.

We would only have four planes left here, and all may not be able to fly. As soon as the first mission returned, they would be readied as soon as possible for a return mission. It was on a where and when needed basis. A lot would depend on what information the returning pilots could provide. All that could be done now was to sit and wait.

About seven, we got a call from the Colonel for all pilots to report to the ready room. Everyone knew it would be about the mission that would be flown the next day. There was still that air of tension but now accompanied by a wave of anticipation.

After we were seated, the Colonel got straight to the point. "We are sure the Viet Minh have been joined by Chinese troops. We think they are at battalion strength, but we are pretty sure they have split them. A lot of this is guesswork and not verified.

Part of the battalion is moving east, which means they will no doubt hit us from the north. The rest are moving more in a southwest direction, which would indicate they will attack from the northwest or west. We do know they have Russian tanks in both groups. We are now, as we speak, rearming our planes with one napalm and one five-hundred-pound high explosive bomb. You will be able to deal with tanks or troops. We will split our eight planes up with one group going north of our position and the other group going to the north and west.

John, be ready for any surprises and make whatever corrections you feel necessary. We want to take out the tanks if possible, so go for them first. You will be in command, so it is your discretion. Do the most damage where it will hurt most."

John was quick to agree with the colonel and addressed the rest of the pilots, asking if they had fully heard and understood what the Colonel had said. All nodded, indicating they understood. John continued, "If you have to, use the napalm on the tanks as well. There are usually a lot of soldiers following the tanks and using them for cover. The napalm can also take out a tank. Use your best judgment and make everything you have count. Your cannons can also destroy the tank tracks, so if you shoot at a tank, try to hit it from the side where the tracks are exposed. Did everybody get that? Anyone got anything to add or questions?" John was greeted with silence.

The Colonel again took over and told the pilots to try to get some rest and be in the ready room at 0500 in the morning. He turned to me and added, "Max, I want you to be here and standing by with the other four planes. Pick the pilots you want with you. John, we will turn your planes around as soon as you land. You may need to go back again. If all your planes are not able to go back, you can fill in with the pilots and Max's planes. Max, you are not to go on any mission unless I personally give you permission. I need either you or John here to help me. Any questions?" There was a deathly silence that filled the room and lingered with only breathing and a few shuffles audible. Everyone got up and left without disturbing the silence.

I knew the night would be long and sleepless for John and the other pilots who were going on the mission. I had done the same thing too many times myself. I felt sure I would not be flying tomorrow, so I did not feel the pressure the other pilots felt. I wanted to go talk to John, but I knew he would have some personal things to do, so I did not want to bother him.

I sat down, thinking I would pen a letter to my parents and perhaps Danny. I stopped and rethought about writing to Danny. She did have another man in her life, so it wasn't right for me to be interfering. I did write to Mom and Dad but only talked about the little things in life. They did not know where I was so I couldn't say anything about what I was doing. I thought it was best that they did not know, it would only worry them.

There was a knock on the door. I was wondering who it could be with all that was happening. I opened the door and found John standing there with a sober look on his face. In a rather muffled voice, he just said, "Mind if I come in?"

I answered, "Of course not, come right in."

"I don't think I could sleep and didn't want to just stare at the wall. I think you know what it's like knowing you're going into battle tomorrow. I've been there before, but I think this one is going to be a tough one."

"They're all tough, John, some just more so than others. Some people say to just not think about it, but you and I know that is entirely impossible. A wise old man told me once that the things we fear most very seldom happen. I guess that really is true in some things, but we have a lot more at stake than losing a ballgame or even some money. I wish I could go with you, John."

"I'm glad you're not, Max. This isn't your battle. You have no reason to put your life on the line for something like this. This is the Legion's battle, not yours."

"John, when the Viet Minh, Chinese, and Russians are trying to take away the rights of some people to live in peace and the way they choose, it is a crime. When they murder them and force them to do things against their will, it is a crime. If they are not stopped, they will continue someplace else. Someone has to stand up for those not able to do it themselves."

"Maybe you're right, Max."

We changed the subject and talked about some of the fun times we had since we met. John and I had formed a very close friendship. It was more like a bond, a bond that could never be broken. I think John left my room feeling better and more prepared for what lay ahead.

0500 the next morning found all the pilots in the ready room. There seemed to be a more relaxed atmosphere throughout the ranks. Maybe it was because the waiting was over. The time had come, and the plan was now in motion.

The Colonel gave everyone a final briefing with little changes. The eight-plane mission would be split into two groups. John would take four planes to the west, and the other four would be led by another officer to the northeast. After expending their bombs and ammunition, they were to return and prepare for another mission, if needed.

Another Legion squadron would alternate their attack with ours and try to keep constant pressure on the enemy forces. I wished John good luck as he left for his plane.

It was now a waiting game. Our planes would maintain radio silence until they reached their targets. They did not want the enemy to be ready for them. It would take about an hour each way to and from the target, with an estimated fifteen or twenty minutes over the target. When they did engage, we would not be able to hear them talking. They would be too far away and too low for the radio signal to reach us. All we could do was to wait and pray for their safety. We would be able to pick up their radio in about an hour and three quarters after they had left here. That should put them about halfway back. They would not give us complete information after the attack so the enemy would not have information on their condition.

We had a little code worked out so they could give us some basic information. If they felt their mission was a success, they would say the sun was shining. If it was a failure, they would say it was overcast. If it was in between, it was partly cloudy. From this, we could have an idea of what we needed to prepare for, or if another mission may be necessary.

If one of the planes was badly damaged and may have to ditch or the pilot bailout, they would say they had a hung bomb. If someone ditched or bailed out, they would say that the bomb came off and give the coordinance so we could send help. This way, the enemy would not know if we had a pilot down.

After the first hour passed, we knew they should be over their target. The next forty-five minutes were very tense. We knew they would have hit their target and had to be about halfway back. We were glued to the radio," anticipating their call. Finally, it came. We had assigned the name to the flights as West and East Flight, and we were Papa.

"This is East Flight calling, Papa."

"Go ahead, East Flight. This is Papa."

"The weather is partly cloudy. We had a hung bomb over the target, and had it come loose at the target. That was the only one."

"Roger, East Flight."

It took another five or six minutes before we heard. "This is West Flight calling, Papa."

"This is Papa, go ahead, West Flight."

"The weather is partly cloudy. I have a hung bomb on my plane. I think I will lose it soon."

"Roger, West leader, keep us informed."

I looked at the colonel and just said, "John."

"Max, get a couple planes in the air and help him."

"Colonel, I'll take Fritz with me."

"Go, Max, I know I can't hold you here with John in trouble."

I was already halfway across the room, yelling for them to get our planes started and ready. Fritz was right behind me.

"Radio silence, Fritz, and just stay close to me and do what I tell you to do."

Fritz just said, "Roger."

I could see one of our plane Captains just starting to turn the engine over. They jumped to life spitting fire and smoke like some angry dragon. He was out of the plane as I jumped onto the wing and into the cockpit. I signaled to pull the wheel chocks as I strapped myself in and hooked up my radio and oxygen.

The plane was rolling in seconds. I looked over at Fritz and gave him the signal to stay close on my wing. I pointed down the taxiway, telling Fritz we would take off from there rather than go to a runway. He nodded his head in acknowledgment. I advanced the throttle to full throttle then pulled it back slightly so Fritz could stay with me. We were in the air in seconds. As I pointed the nose up, I reduced the throttle a little and adjusted my RPM for best climbing speed. I altered our course slightly and was already passing through 10,000 feet.

"Tower can you give me a true heading to...."

I didn't want to say West Flight and didn't have to. The flight controller just said 330.

Just then, John came up on the radio. "I'm going to have to drop this hung bomb soon."

I had my Birddog direction finder on and picked John up. That gave me another true heading to where he was.

I came up on the radio and just asked. "John, what is your angels?" Which was asking him his altitude.

I just heard a quick eight. This meant John was at eight thousand feet. I needed to get a more accurate fix on John without alerting the enemy he was going down. "John, did you know today is my birthday? Can you sing me a happy birthday song?"

John followed with a wonderful rendition of "Happy Birthday." I had already turned my bird dog on (radio direction finder) and had a quick direction to him. I had started to descend as soon as I knew he was below us. The bird dog gave me the direction I needed to follow to find John. I picked him up in a few minutes and headed for him. As I circled and closed in on him, I could see he had a lot of damage and trailing a thin line of vapor which appeared to be fuel. As I joined up on his left wing, I patted my head and pointed to myself, which told the rest of his flight that I had the lead.

I waved to them and pointed toward our home field, which told them to go home. I knew they were getting low on fuel and perhaps had some damage. I wanted them to get home and get on the ground as quickly as possible. Fritz was close on my wing. I held my closed fist sideways with my thumb stuck straight out and rotated it up and down, which was asking him his condition. John returned with a similar jester telling me he had some problems but not really bad. A thumbs up would have told me he was good, a thumbs down would have indicated he had injuries.

After continuing a short distance, John's engine quit, and I could see the prop was just windmilling in the wind. John immediately started to lose altitude. I quickly called Papa, gave them the coordinance and informed them that the hung bomb had come loose and was falling toward the earth. I quickly signaled Fritz with my index finger straight up and moving in a circular motion followed by pointing down in the direction we were going.

Fritz nodded his head, broke off, and headed down ahead of us. He knew I wanted him to check the area John would land in to see if any of the enemy were in the area.

John started to maneuver, trying to reach a small clearing in the jungle. I looked over in time to see Fritz drop a napalm bomb a short distance away. I was sure he had located some of the enemy and was trying to suppress them. As we continued down, I was intent on following John and was startled when Fritz passed directly in front of us with his guns blazing.

There was little doubt that we had enemy very near to where John would land. I watched as John contacted the ground with his wheels up and skidded to a stop in some brush. I pulled up and tried to see if he exited the plane. John was slumped over in the cockpit. He had collided with a tree which must have rendered him unconscious. At the same time, I noticed soldiers entering the far side of the clearing, so I turned toward them and released my napalm bomb as I passed over them. I pulled up, reversed, and made another run, dropping my 500-pound bomb. The soldiers were retreating rapidly, so I encouraged them with my cannons on my next run. Fritz was also working an area close by.

On my following pass, I noticed that John had not moved and was still in his plane. I again put my cannons to work to discourage the enemy from approaching any closer. As I pulled up my plane was struck by heavy machine-gun fire, and black smoke immediately erupted from the engine cowling. I only had time to turn back to the clearing and bellied in, stopping within about fifty yards of John and his plane. I exited my plane and made a dash for John. John had recovered consciousness and was starting to get out of his plane. Mine was in flames. I think John hit the ground running.

We made a dash for some heavy jungle and kept going as the foliage relentlessly tore at our skin and clothing. I knew we were both bleeding as we continued through the jungle. We reached a small river and immediately plunged into it, swimming toward the other side.

I looked back long enough to see that two more F8s had joined Fritz and were pounding our pursuers relentlessly. That was enough of a deterrent for them to call off their chase, retreating back into the jungle.

When John and I reached the other side of the river, we kept going for as long as we could. Finally, exhausted, we stopped to rest. We looked at each other. John just smiled and said, "Happy birthday, Max. I didn't have time to pick up a present."

"I should have known, the parties over then. Let's go home."

"Lead the way, I'll follow you." That bit of humor seemed to release some of the tension.

CHAPTER XI

We decided to continue on through the jungle while we still had some daylight. If we could, we wanted to get as far away as possible. After traveling a short distance, we found a freshwater stream which afforded us some rather cool water to drink. There was also some fruit on a nearby tree that resembled a ball of sorts, so we tried it. It didn't have a bad taste, but not being sure, we ate just a small amount to see if it would have an adverse effect on us. We knew we had to get some rest, so we climbed into a tree and braced ourselves between a couple of limbs to keep from falling out.

We had both expressed our feelings that we didn't want some tiger or other wild animals to have us for dinner. I asked John if he knew if there were any other large cats in the jungle that may climb up and get us. John looked a little startled and said, "Did you have to mention something like that? I was just getting to feel safe."

"Don't worry, John, there is no doubt some very large snakes living in the trees that will scare them away."

"I would also like to thank you for that bit of information. Goodnight."

"Goodnight, John, pleasant dreams."

We both knew that the Viet Minh would be looking for us, so we would have to keep moving to stay ahead of them. Neither of us thought they would try to move through the heavy brush and rugged terrain at night. That was almost impossible. We felt rather secure in stopping for the night, but we knew we would have to get moving at first light.

As John came down from our tree in the morning, I greeted him with, "Good morning, John, I see you avoided the tigers and large snakes last night."

"Don't talk about snakes or spiders, I hate both."

I don't think either one of us had gotten much rest during the night. Being stuck in the crotch of a tree was not very conducive to sleep. When we woke up in the morning, we had to formulate a plan and not just start out blindly. We took the time to do that as we started walking.

We knew we had to go to the southwest to reach friendly territory, so we calculated that we were about a hundred miles from our base, about half in enemy territory. The other half would, no doubt, have enemy patrols in it as well. One never knew just who the Viet Minh were. They could be farmers one day and soldiers the next. All we had for protection were the revolvers we carried in a shoulder harness. They would not be much help against rifles, machine guns, and larger weapons. It was imperative that we avoid contact. The fruit we had eaten the night before seemed to have agreed with us, so we ate more of that and drank water out of the stream. The water in the stream appeared to be very clear, so we decided it would be alright to drink. We were fortunate that neither of us had received any injuries, and we both had on good boots. It was essential that we find something to eat and drink as we traveled. We had nothing to carry water in, so that did present a problem.

"Max, I think we should try to follow this stream since it is going in the general direction we have to go. It will help us not to leave tracks, and we will have water to drink."

"I think that sounds like a good idea. If they, the Viet Minh, don't outguess us and expect us to do that."

John thought a while. "Maybe we could make it look like we left the river by walking up the bank and then walking backward in our same tracks and into the water again."

"I'm willing to try anything, and that does sound like it might work. At least we will always think it should. There is still the possibility that the Colonel will try to find us. If Fritz made it back, he could give them an idea where we may be. If he went down without giving his position, it would be difficult to search for him or us. If they found our planes, they would have an idea of which way we would be traveling. That would be toward our base."

"Max, I would like to give that thought more credibility, but there are too many unknown factors." John looked at me with a very inquisitive look on his face. "Max, did you keep any of the flares in your life jacket? I never thought to keep mine and tossed them away. They would come in handy if our people did show up."

"I did put the two I had in one of my flight suit pockets. One end is a flare for at night, the other end is an orange smoke for daylight. We have those if we need them."

We followed the stream for about a mile when it abruptly turned to the south. There was no choice but to leave it. After we did leave, we would come to clearings occasionally which we avoided other than to stay on the edge so we could slip back into the foliage if necessary.

On the third day, we were following the edge of a clearing when we came to a road. It was evident that the road was well traveled. John asked if I thought we were in friendly territory yet. I told him I thought we were, at best, in a sort of no man's land. I felt we had more chance to run into Viet Minh than we did the Legion. I knew that both sides had patrols operating in the area between the positions held by each side. Small patrols would indicate a kind of no man's land while larger units would indicate territory that was held by those forces. Cautiously we tried to look down the road in either direction but did not see or hear anything. It would be necessary for us to cross a large clearing on the other side of the road, so we had to be very sure we would not let any of the enemy see or hear us. We crouched there waiting for something. Not sure what we were waiting for. Perhaps just to get our courage up to step out onto the road. Suddenly John grabbed the clothing on my left shoulder to stop or warn me, I wasn't sure which. "I hear something, Max. Do you hear it?" There was an unmistakable sound of a thud, thud that was the sound of a chopper.

"I hear it, John. It can only be a chopper, and the Viet Minh doesn't have any choppers in this area. I am sure it is one of ours."

John excitedly blurted out. "Get your flare out, get your flare out!"

I tossed John a flare and said. "You light the night flair, and I'll do the smoke. Give them everything we have; this may be our only chance."

Both of us ran out into the clearing, setting our flares off and waving our arms as hard as we could. The choppers seemed to hesitate and stop in midair. Then turned and came back directly at us. Suddenly they unleashed a hail of machine-gun fire which looked like it was meant for us. John and I hit the ground in disbelief. John yelled, "Why are they shooting at us? Don't they know who we are?"

I was as confused as John was until I looked behind us. From the brush, I could see the flash of gunfire. The firing from both directions continued briefly. We had undoubtedly encountered a small patrol. Suddenly it stopped, allowing the chopper to set down about fifty yards from us. I could see someone motioning for us to come. John and I both, without hesitation, started for the chopper. The gunner in the chopper started to fire over our heads, which I felt was very close to us. I covered the ground between the chopper and us in Olympic time. I grasped the hand of the man standing at the doorway and propelled myself inside. As I looked back. John was not there. I looked again and could see he was down only about thirty yards away. The chopper started to lift off. I turned, grabbed the carbine rifle from the Legion soldier, and jumped back onto the ground. I could hear someone yelling, "Get on board, get on board! He is down we need to leave."

I just shouted back, "Then go." I would not leave John. We either went together or stayed together. I would never leave him if I thought he was still alive. The chopper lifted off. I reached John and could see he was hit but still alive. John just looked at me and shouted, "Get out of here while you can."

"Why didn't you tell me that sooner, I think I missed my ride." I looked around and could see the chopper coming back in with guns covering the bush where the fire had come from. The return fire was light, which meant most of the resistance was eliminated.

As the chopper settled down to land, I helped John to his feet and carried or dragged him toward the chopper. We were helped into the chopper. I let go of John and let him down on the deck. This was the first time I could see how badly he was injured. I could see blood around his right shoulder and more on the outside of his right leg. The soldier quickly cut John's clothing away to reach the wounds. The wound in the right shoulder was centered in his shoulder blade, while the leg wounds had penetrated close to the bone and appeared to have missed the bone itself. It was not life-threatening. I offered my thanks for that with a quick prayer. They gave John some shots of Morphine which sent him into another world. He seemed to relax and ignore the pain and discomfort.

As we continued back to our base, one of the crewmen was trying to put compression bandages on John's wounds, trying to stop or slow down the bleeding. John was drifting in and out of consciousness, trying to talk to us but not making much sense. When we hit the ground, John was quickly carried off to the hospital so he could get the attention he needed. I was informed the Colonel wanted to see me, so I headed for his office.

As I entered his office, I offered a salute and stated that I was reporting as ordered. "Sit down, Max. I never thought I would see you or John again. I can't tell you how happy I am. You have been out of communication with the rest of the world, so you don't know what has taken place.

Our forces at Dien Bien Phu have surrendered to the Viet Minh. It is one of the most devastating defeats the Legion has ever experienced. There was no way out, so all our forces had to surrender. Some five thousand men in all. They are all prisoners and being marched into confinement. We know many will not survive, and there is nothing we can do. We had no way of getting them out.

We surrendered to try to save those that were still alive. Time will tell if it was the right decision. We feel that the Viet Minh will turn toward our base, so it will be evacuated as soon as possible. We simply do not have the ability to fight back. Of the twelve planes and fifteen pilots we had in our squadron when we arrived, we have only five planes left. We have lost three pilots, and two are missing. Fritz, after he left you and John, had a plane so badly damaged he had to bail out without giving us any information. He broke his ankle on the tail as he left the airplane. I don't know how he did it, but he walked for three days on a broken ankle before being picked up and brought back to the field.

It was only then that we learned you and John may still be alive. We were lucky even to find you. We will leave here as soon as possible and take what we can to another Legion base. We are not sure where that is at this time. We intend to take the remaining F8s with us.

You and John will leave with me tomorrow or the next day by air. Many will have to travel by land. Max, I want to thank you for your service in the Legion. This is my personal thanks; I am sure you will hear much more. You have upheld the honor of the Legion and set standards for all Legionnaire to follow. It has been an honor and privilege to have served with you." With that, the Colonel stood up and offered a salute.

After returning the salute, I offered, "The honor has been mine, sir. To serve with men like you and John is a privilege not found by many. Thank you for allowing this."

We shook hands, and I departed to check on John. I found that John was still in surgery, so I waited for him. I was told that it could be another hour or two, so I went back to my room to cleaned up. I returned to the surgical room where John was, grabbed a cup of coffee and sat down to wait. It gave me time to think about all that had happened. It seemed that my time in Korea and in a North Korean prison was in a different lifetime. Like I was looking at a different person in a different life. I wondered if I even knew this person.

The door opened to the waiting room I was in, and a young nurse stepped out. "Are you Commander Bradly?" I said I was, she smiled and said that someone wanted to see me. I stood up and followed her. As we stopped just outside another room, she turned and said, "Your friend is still under a little sedation but will come out of it soon." I thanked her and stepped into the room with John.

He looked at me and tried to say something. His words were slurred and broken. He wasn't making sense in anything he said, so I just patted him on the shoulder and told him to try to rest for a few minutes. He closed his eyes and seemed to drift off for a while. I leaned back and enjoyed the silence.

I couldn't help but think about all that had happened in the past. I thought about the men I flew with in Korea. The men who lost their lives just trying to destroy a bridge. I wondered what difference it made now. I wondered if the bridges had been rebuilt or if they were still in ruins just as we had left them. I, again, thought about the men who died trying to destroy them, and the families that will mourn and cry for them the rest of their lives. I thought about the children who would never see their fathers again. Of the wives having to raise their children, trying to be both mother and father. The sons without a father to be with them in the Boy Scouts, or to cheer them on in the big football or other ball games. I thought about the daughters who would never have a father to dance with on some special occasion, or to introduce to their first boyfriend. I thought about the women lying in their bed at night, dampening their pillows with the tears they shed in loneliness. They would never again hear their loved one speak the soft words of, "I love you," or have someone to hold their hand when they are sad. They would feel the loneliness that comes in the dark hours of the night.

Some will find someone else to take the place of the loved one they lost, but not all. Even though they do, they will always remember and be sad.

I thought of Sarah and what it would be like to be married to someone like her. You would always have to walk in her shadow and be considered lucky to have married someone so famous. It was difficult for me not to think a marriage like that would be like a puppet on a string. When she pulled the string, you reacted and did her bidding. One day she may become weary and tired of pulling that string and say, "I want to cut that string and be free of you, I want a new string to hold." I knew it would almost be inevitable for this to happen. It was like a roadmap in front of you. She may plead her feelings and undying love for you now, but it would be very likely to happen. The future is best judged by the past. She has already been married twice before. The map is spread out in front of you and very unlikely to change. I remembered the old saying that a leopard cannot change its spots.

I like Sarah, but I would not allow that to happen. I paused for just a few seconds and sort of laughed. I almost said out loud, I like Sarah, but I don't think I love her, and love is necessary."

I was suddenly jolted back to reality when John just said, "Max." I looked over at John and was greeted with a big smile. I just said, "Hi, John, welcome back, I thought I may have lost you earlier."

"I didn't have a chance to thank you, Max. If you had not come back for me, I wouldn't be here now. I knew I was hit pretty hard when I went down. I really thought that was the end. I had little doubt; I wrote myself off. You risk your life for me, and you weren't even sure I was alive. What made you do that?"

"I guess I'm not sure why. Maybe I can best explain it in a few words by just saying that you're my friend. That and I knew you would have come back for me."

"Let's not put me to the test, I'm not sure I would have had the courage."

"John, your courage is something I would never question. Did you hear about the Legion surrendering?"

"I did. I know they would never surrender if they thought they had a fighting chance. I have met the officer in charge of the operation, and he is not one to surrender if he has any chance at all. I am sure he did it to save lives. That sometimes takes more courage than to keep on fighting."

"Our squadron didn't fare too well either, did you hear about that?"

"No, I didn't, Max."

"We lost seven of our twelve planes. Also, three pilots and two more missing. We are pulling out of our base here in the next day or two. We will fly the remaining F8s out with us. You and I will go with the Colonel. Not sure where we will go. Don't think the Colonel knows himself. Just need to pull back and see what happens."

John asked, "Do you know who the pilots were that we lost and are missing?"

"The Colonel never said. I didn't ask, I knew he had a lot of things on his mind and I didn't want to bother him any more than was necessary. Are you feeling well enough to travel, John?"

"Don't think I have a choice. My shoulder is giving me most of my trouble. There is not much they can do about this cast. It's just plain bad the way it sticks up. I'll just have to make do with what I have."

"I think I'm going to try to get some rest, John. It's been an interesting day, and I'm just plain tired. Think I'll try to get something to eat. Can I get you anything and bring it back to you?"

"I am sure they will take care of me here with whatever I need. Keep me up to date on what is happening. And, Max, I could never repay you for what you did today. I think you know that I am indebted to you. I think you also know that you have a friend that you can call on anytime for anything."

"John, I think that already was the case for both of us. Get some rest, I'll see you in the morning."

The next morning, I made my appearance in our ready room and found the Colonel already there. When he saw me, he walked over to me and said. "Max, we had a report come in that one of our transport planes think they saw someone trying to signal them just inside the enemy held territory to our northeast. We think it may be one of our pilots that went down a few days ago. We have a good fix on the location where the sighting was made. I need someone responsible and familiar with such a situation to go in and check it out. I hate to ask you to do this, and you can turn me down if you want."

I never let him finish. I just said, "Give me another pilot to go with me."

"Pick whoever you want. I'll get all the information you will need. We'll have a chopper standing by that you can call in if you find him. We only surrendered the troops at Dien Bien Phu. We are still able to take whatever action you may think necessary in this area. We know the Viet Minh will try to kill our pilot if they can get to him. If you find him send back a coded signal for the chopper to aid you."

I acknowledged the Colonel and continued, "Let's get a map, so you can give me the location they last saw him in. We know there are enemy troops in that area. I found that out firsthand. You may want to have a couple more F8s standing by. We may need them if we run into a larger force of the enemy. The Viet Minh have had time to move some of their troops from Dien Bien Phu into our area. This would be true, especially if they are thinking about an assault on our airfield. I think that would be logical to expect. They have had one victory and ready for another. Have you given the order to have planes ready for us?"

"That's being done right now. Who do you want to go with you?"

"I know Fritz can't fly with a broken ankle, is Dutch still with us?"

"He is," the Colonel quickly replied.

"I'll take him."

"Who do you want for backup pilots?"

"Pick anyone, they are all good."

The colonel turned to a junior officer who was with him and told him to see that the orders were carried out. The junior officer offered an acknowledgment of the order and left the room.

The Colonel rolled out a map on a table and started searching for the location. "Max, we received the information that he was here yesterday," he said as he put his finger on the map. "I would expect him to continue toward our base if he is able. I do not have a report on his condition so you can draw a line toward where we are and expect him to be on or near that line.

Your planes will not have bombs since we don't have time to hang them. Your cannons will have to do. Max, don't take any unnecessary chances if you can avoid it. If it is one of our pilots, we want him back, but I also don't want anything to happen to you. I hate to send you on this mission, but you're the best I have. We need to, if it is one of our pilots, get him back and move out of here."

"I'll do the best I can, Colonel."

"I know you will, thank you."

As we finished talking, Dutch walked into the room. I gave him a quick briefing as we got into our flight suits and other gear. The planes were ready. As I was getting into the plane, I remembered we had not set up a code phrase to tell them if it was one of our pilots and for the chopper to be launched. I motioned for the plane Captain to jump up on the wing and talk to me. I scratched a note on my knee pad, tore it off, and told him to give it to the Colonel as soon as possible and without fail. I told the Colonel that I would call and use this code if I found our man. I would simply say the birthday cake has one or more candles if there were more men. If I told him to light the candles at two o'clock, he was to launch the chopper in that direction to get to us. I signaled the plane Captain to pull the chocks away from the wheels.

After he did, he signaled me. I was clear to taxi. I started to move toward the runway with Dutch right behind me. We made a formation takeoff and took up a heading to where our man was last sighted.

It only took about twenty minutes to reach the coordinate where the sighting was made. I took us down to five hundred feet and set up a search pattern. It only took about ten minutes before we saw some smoke on the ground. I took us down to treetop level and flew over the smoke.

On the ground was someone jumping up and down and waving their arms. There was no mistake, it was one of our pilots still in his flight suit. I quickly called our base and told them the birthday cake had one candle and to light it at two-thirty. All I heard back was an acknowledgment saying that they had it and would comply. Now, all we had to do was wait.

As we were waiting for the chopper, I noticed some smoke or dust a few miles to the north. I took us up to three thousand feet and headed in that direction. As we neared it, I saw it was dust from a column of vehicles. We started to draw some light fire from weapons that had tracers in them, which told us they were not just rifles. We knew who they were and that they were attracted by our presence and were headed toward us. I climbed to a higher altitude and headed away from our pilot trying to draw them away from him.

If our plan was working, they would not know about the downed pilot, so I headed to the north to get them to turn in that direction. I called the base. "This is the birthday boy; we have guests arriving for the party. Dutch and I will go see that they have a proper greeting. The party is still on, so keep the rest of the guests coming."

As we turned to the north, the column stopped. The firing had stopped since we were out of range. I called Dutch. "Dutch, let's see that our friends have a proper invitation. You start at the head of the column, and I'll start at the rear. That way they can't fire in two directions at once.

If you lose sight of me, break right before you reach the middle of the column, and I will do the same. Pull up and come back in the opposite direction of your first run and do the same thing as before. Let me know when you are in position."

In a short time, I heard Dutch tell me he was in position. "OK, start your run." I rolled into a shallow dive and started my run. As I approached the column, I could see that there were trees on both sides of the column, preventing them from getting their vehicles off the road. The men were bailing out of the vehicles and running for the trees. I knew they would only have small arms and machine guns with them. I quickly called Dutch and told him to concentrate on the vehicles rather than the troops. I knew if we could destroy their vehicles and block the road they could not, on foot, get to our man on the ground in time to interfere with the pickup. I had Dutch in sight and broke right before we reached the center of the column. As I looked over my shoulder, I could see damaged and burning vehicles throughout the column. I got on the radio. "Dutch, hold off on your next run. I don't think there is much left." We were drawing gunfire, so I told Dutch to join on me. I moved us out of range of the gunfire and called the base.

"How is the birthday party going? We send an invitation to some uninvited guests. I think they have decided not to come to the party."

"That's too bad, we are just now picking up the birthday boy and will have him on the way home in a few minutes."

"Roger, let me know when the party's over."

"Will do."

Dutch and I did not want to go to where the pickup was taking place until they had him. We did not want to draw attention to them if they had a delay. In about ten minutes we heard, "the party is over, we are on our way home."

"We'll stay with you until you get home. Dutch have any damage?"

"I did take some machinegun fire. The plane is OK, but I took a hit in my right leg. I used my scarf to make a tourniquet."

I blurted out on the radio. "Chopper, we're leaving, got to get Dutch home. Stay with me, Dutch, I'm taking us home as fast as I can. Do you feel OK? Are you losing a lot of blood? Do you feel lightheaded?"

"Max, I'm controlling the blood flow. I don't think I am losing that much."

"Keep talking to me, Dutch, if you start to feel light-headed, we will set you down somewhere."

The next twenty minutes were filled with anxiety. I had all the power on our engines I thought they could stand. I was not going to lose Dutch this late in the game. Finally, I saw the field. "The field's just ahead of us, you go in first and stop as soon as you can and cut your engine. You still doing OK?"

"I feel a little woozy, but I am still OK."

"Get on the ground as soon as you can. Tower get someone out there now."

"We have an ambulance on the way."

I looked down at my hand I had on the throttle, it was shaking. I knew someone was telling me something, and I better listen. I watched as Dutch touched down and rolled out. I flew past him and could see he was starting to slump forward. I saw his prop slowly stop turning and the plane coast to a stop. I knew it had been very close. I said a prayer and added many things. I asked to be forgiven for all the things I had to do and that I would never have to see combat again. I knew I had fought for what is right in this world. I knew I could never fly in combat again. Someone else would have to right all the wrongs in this world. I was not sure I ever wanted to fly again.

I landed and taxied to the hanger. The Colonel was there to greet me. I know he wanted to congratulate me. When he looked at me, the smile on his face disappeared. He just looked at me and said. "Max, we better get you inside, you don't look very good. Are you injured?"

"No sir, I am not injured. I came very near to losing Dutch today. Another ten minutes and I don't think he would have survived. He was starting to slur his words. I should have asked him sooner if he had any injuries. It would have been my fault. I think I'm getting tired, Colonel, very tired."

"Max, you have been through a lot today. I think you need just to sit down and relax for a while. Try to forget about all the tension. Try to shut the day out and think about something else. You got Dutch back. If you had not been with Dutch to help him, I am sure he would not be here right now. Be thankful that you did help him."

"Maybe your right, Colonel. I think I'll go see how he is doing. He should have told me sooner that he had been wounded. Just too proud to complain. Maybe he learned something today. I hope he did."

The Colonel looked at me. "Want me to go along?"

"No, I want to see John too, and that could drag on for a while."

"OK, we will be leaving in the morning, so have your things ready to go."

I found Dutch still in the surgical room. He had some metal in the wound that had to come out. It was in pretty deep and was giving the doctor a hard time. Dutch was getting a transfusion and was back to full consciousness. As I walked in, the doctor finally managed to get the metal out. Dutch just laid back and said. "I'm glad that finally came out."

I asked, "How you are getting along, is the Doc treating you right?"

"He is doing a good job, just had some metal that was giving him a hard time."

"Dutch, you should have told me sooner about being wounded. That could have cost you your life. Whether you realize it or not, you came pretty near to making that your last mission."

"Max, I didn't realize it was that bad. If I had known, I would have done things differently. Thanks for getting me back. You're the reason I did get back, Thank you."

"You're very welcome. I'm glad I could help. Now, just don't do it again."

John wasn't too far away, so I thought I would check on him to see how he was doing. He was having quite a time trying to write a letter with his left hand. As I walked in, he just put down his pen and looked at me. "Well, here comes the conquering hero. They tell me you had a very busy day. Glad you made it back, I was in no mood to go to a funeral."

"No one was happier than me that you didn't have to go to a funeral. I think Dutch was the one that came close. He had a bad wound and never told me until it was almost too late. He is the lucky one to be alive. How are you doing? I see you can't write with your left hand. Want some help?"

"No, it is private, and I am afraid you may read it. They tell me we will be leaving in the morning."

"That's what the Colonel told me. I think we better leave, the Viet Minh are getting closer."

John added. "I wonder who will get blamed for all the losses we had. It had to be a blunder on someone's part."

"Sure hope it's not you or me, John. I am really tired; think I will turn in and get some rest. Tomorrow could be another busy day. Goodnight."

"Goodnight, Max, see you in the morning."

CHAPTER XII

woke up at five and couldn't get back to sleep, so I thought I may as well get up. I made my way to the mess hall and begged for a cup of coffee. Someone took pity on me, even though they were not open, and gave me one.

I felt a lot better than I did last evening. That had been a very tough day, certainly one that I won't forget for a very long time. I thought about going over and seeing if John was awake but figured he needed his rest, so I discarded that idea. I hung out at the mess for about half an hour, then decided to see if the Colonel was up. I walked over to his quarters. I could see that he was up, so I knocked on the door. I heard a, "Come in," so I did. After exchanging a good morning, he asked if I had my gear ready so it could be picked up. I told him I did. He said we would leave in about two hours, and to have someone get it to our plane.

I asked where we would be going. "Saigon will be our first stop. After that, I am not sure. We should be back in France soon. I am sure we will be asked a lot of questions when we get there. We should not be in the hot seat since we were not in on the decision making. I think you will be able to go home whenever you want. If you want to spend some time in France, I am sure that will be up to you. You should also be able to arrange how you want to be paid. Just let me know if I can help in any way."

"I will do that. I think I may spend a little time with John before I go home. It may be a long time before I see him again."

After I left the Colonel, I walked over to where John was. He was setting up in bed, eating his breakfast. I was greeted with. "Good morning, Max, you look a little more jovial than you did the last time I saw you. You must be feeling better."

"Matter of fact I do. Yesterday was a tough day. I was exhausted after the mission and almost losing Dutch. That was much to close."

"Max, you never did tell me what happened. I only know that Dutch was wounded. What else went on?"

"I didn't know that Dutch had been wounded in our attack. He never bothered to tell me until we were starting back. He had used his scarf for a tourniquet to try to stop the bleeding. He thought he had it stopped, but he must not have. When I found out, I went all out to get him home before he passed out. We just barely made it. I think he lost a lot of consciousness on the rollout after he landed. Another ten minutes and I am not sure he could have made the landing. I tried to keep him talking, so if I did think he was passing out, I would try to get him down in a field. When he did go out, it happened fast. I'm not sure I would have been able to talk him into a field."

"Everyone has to learn sometime and somehow. The bad part of it is that the lesson can be fatal." John hesitated and continued. "Who was the pilot they picked up?"

"I never found out, John. Guess I never even thought to ask. I don't even know what kind of condition he was in or how long he had been missing."

John replied, "He didn't come into the hospital here, so he must not have been in too bad of a condition."

I changed the subject. "Have you got your gear ready to go? I think we will be leaving soon. The Colonel said our first stop would be Saigon. The Viet Minh are really close to Saigon, so I don't care to hang around there very long."

"I still need to get my gear together, not sure when I can do that."

"If you let me have your key, I can get it together. You got a duffel bag or something I can put it in?"

"There's a couple parachute bags under the bed you can use. There's nothing too frail so just throw it in any way you can. You'll find the key under the door matt."

"Now that's what I call original, I am sure no one would think to look there."

"OK, Max, so I was in a hurry."

"I'm going over to the mess hall and get something to eat before I go over to your room. I'll get someone to haul both our stuff to the plane. I am sure you will get a ride over. If I don't see you there, I will see that you do get there."

"I'll see you at the plane, Max."

"OK, see you later."

At the mess hall, I saw the Colonel who told me that the plane would leave at 0900. It was now 0730. I quickly ate and hurried over to John's room. On the way, I told the duty officer to have someone over to our building as soon as he could.

The transportation arrived on schedule. I loaded everything up and headed for our plane with fifteen minutes to spare. The rest of the pilots from our squadron who would not be flying one of our planes would go with us as well as some other officers. The atmosphere was rather sober. We were leaving with less than a jubilant departure.

The fight to Saigon was uneventful. It did give all of us pilots the opportunity to compare notes and experiences. I found the pilot that we had helped rescue had been lost for about three days before he was able to make contact with someone. His name was Mike, he was from England. I know he had a story in his background that might be a little shady. However, nothing was asked, and nothing was offered, so we just accepted him, maybe because we liked his smile. I think it was because it was none of our business. That is the rule of the Legion. I never met a Legionnaire I didn't like nor one I couldn't trust in battle. Their private life was just that, private.

When we landed in Saigon, we never left the plane. It was refueled and back into the air. I was wondering where are remaining F8s had gone. I never asked, just figured it was none of my business.

John was a little uncomfortable with his right shoulder and arm in a cast. I know the wounds in his leg caused him a lot of discomforts also. The two of us spent a lot of time talking. It was never brought up, but it looked doubtful to me that John would be able to fly again. I think he knew it and just didn't want to talk about it. He expressed his feelings for Adele and thought he might be ready to make a major move in his life. That is the way he put it. I think he was just afraid to say marriage. I told him that if that major move included Adele, he couldn't make a better move. If ever two people should be together, it would be John and Adele. I risked saying that. Surprisingly, John agreed and even with a smile. He asked me what I thought of Sarah. I told him the truth. She would have made a wonderful partner in life if she had not experienced so much fame.

"I think you could change her, Max. She has really fallen for you. I know she would not try to lead you around on a rope as many would. I think you are the only man I know that could continue always to be her equal. I don't mean that in a derogatory way. That's just the way a marriage should work. I always felt marriage should not be thought of in terms of me and you. It should always be thought of in terms of us."

"I wish I could agree with you, John. Her track record is not that great. She has had two marriages, and she is not that old. I am sure each of her marriages started with a promise of undying love. She would have just too many offers from guys to escape into a new magical world of love. It must have happened twice before. I don't want to be a part of the third time."

"Maybe your right, Max. I can see your point. It's just that I have known her for a long time. She and Adele were friends before she arrived at the lofty position she is at now. I have dated Adele most of that time. Adele told me she has never seen Sarah fall for someone so hard as she has you. I guess I would feel the same way you do, they say history repeats itself. That is very true, but it is also true that there are exceptions. I think you can tell I like Sarah and I would like to see you two together. It must be your decision. You can't just walk away from that kind of a mistake if it is a mistake."

"John, have I ever told you about a girl named Danny?"

"I don't recall hearing that name."

"When I was shot down the first time in Korea, I was taken to an Army hospital. I met a girl there, an Army Nurse, who I thought was an angel. We had a little rough start, but I fell for her like I never thought possible. I couldn't explain it if I tried for a thousand years. I only know I have never been so sure of anything in my life about anyone. I think she felt the same as I did. Even after meeting and being with her for such a short time, I knew I would never want any other girl for as long as I lived.

I was shot down again and reported dead. She had no way of knowing I was still alive. I spent almost an entire year in a North Korean prison, not knowing I had been listed as dead. I can't blame her for accepting that and looking for someone else. I think she may be engaged now, I'm not really sure. I was hurt, and I wasn't very nice to her. I never gave her a chance to explain, I just went on the offensive. I didn't want to see or hear from her again, and I think I told her that. She and my Mom have gotten to know each other. I think my mom is angry with me for the way I acted. She is all I thought about all the while I was a prisoner in Korea. I think that is what kept me going." I stopped and told John I was sorry for unloading my trouble on him and fell silent.

"Max, I don't mind being a sounding board. That's what friends are for."

"Take my advice, John, and don't let Adele get away. I don't think they come any better than Adele."

164

"That's good advice, Max, I plan on doing that if she will have me. I was hoping you would stay long enough to be my best man if she does say yes."

"I would be honored. If I must come back, I will."

One of the pilots came back and talked to the Colonel. The Colonel stood up and announced that we would be landing in a few minutes. We would spend the night here and continue on to France in the morning. No one even asked where we were. I didn't think anyone even cared. Later we found out we were on some island I had never heard of before. We were all happy to get some food and take a break from flying. John was taken to a hospital of sorts along with Dutch so they could get their bandages changed. They both stayed there overnight.

The following morning, we had some breakfast, boarded the plane, and were off once again. The Colonel invited John and me to sit with him. The conversation was centered around the Legion's surrender, and what mistakes were made along with a guess about who made them. The rest of the conversation was centered around our families.

We did stop once more to refuel and pick up some food. We were not on the ground very long. I did go up and fly for a while. The other pilots had been taking turns, so I thought I should help a bit also.

It was late in the evening when we finally landed at our old base in France. John and Dutch stayed at the hospital again while we grabbed some blankets and stayed in a convenient barracks. We ate some sandwiches before we turned in.

The following day was a casual day for most of us. The Colonel and John were asked to appear before a board of inquiry. The board had been convened to try and put the puzzle of why they lost together.

That afternoon, John found time to call Adele. She had no idea that we were back. She knew about the Legion surrender, but that was all. John did not tell her he had been wounded. He was worried that she would panic and want to see him right away. The hospital still did not want John running around with his wounds still needing time to heal. He had told Adele that he had to stay on the base, and I would pick her up. He approached me and told me what he wanted me to say.

"Max, I told Adele that I was not able to leave the base and that you would pick her up and bring her here. She has a tendency to get excited sometimes. Will you kind of break it to her that I did get hurt a little and the Doctor wants me to stay on the base? I asked her not to bring Sarah."

"I will tell her anything you want me to. I think she already knows something is not just right. Did she question you when you told her not to bring Sarah?"

"Not really, she is not pushy. She knows something is different and will leave it go for now."

I told John that I wanted to find my room and get settled if I could, so I left for my old room to see if my gear was there. I had only been there a short time when a young soldier knocked on my door. I answered it and was handed a message with the explanation that this had come into the duty officer with a request to deliver it to me. I wasn't sure who it would be from, I thought maybe Sarah if Adele had talked to her. I opened it and found only two words, they were, "Call Me." I knew Adele must be upset and knew something was wrong. I hurried to the nearest phone I could find and called Adele. I heard a, "hello," on the other end. I tried to be as unconcerned as I could when I answered back.

"This is Max. Adele, what can I do for you?"

"Max, what is going on? I know somethings wrong with John. I'm worried sick, is he dying? Is he hurt badly? Why can't he pick me up?"

"Wow! Settle down, Adele, John is OK." Adele was starting to cry now. She wanted to say something but was sobbing too much to even speak. "Adele, believe me, John is OK. Can you stop long enough for me to say something?" I could still hear the sniffling and what sounded like she was trying to catch her breath.

"Are you able to listen to me, Adele?"

"I'm alright now, Max, sorry."

"I will make it plain and simple. John was wounded, but the wounds are not life-threatening. He will make a full recovery. I think he may have some restrictions, but he will be OK."

Adele started to cry again. "For Pete's sake, Adele, stop crying, and listen to me."

"I'm sorry, Max, I just love him so much. Please tell me what happened."

"John was on a mission; he ran into heavy gunfire and had his plane damaged rather badly. I tried to go help him, but he went down, still in enemy territory. I was shot down also and crashed near John. We both escaped without injuries. We spent three days trying to make it back. When they picked us up, while getting to the chopper, John took three bullets, one in his shoulder and two in his leg. He did make it to the chopper, and we made it out.

None of the wounds are life-threatening, but it will take time to recover. Adele, you can be very proud of John. He is a very brave man. I will tell you this because I think you need to know. I think John knows that the shoulder wound will possibly keep him from flying again. It will be hard for him to accept that. I am sure he knows, but he does not want to talk about it. I think you know what I am trying to tell you. Don't push him. Let him bring it up. He will when he is ready. Adele, I may be stepping over the limits of what I should say. John and I had a long talk. Mostly about you. He may feel as though he is less of a man if he can't return to flying, and that could make him feel inferior. He loves you, Adele, and even more, he needs you. Don't ever offer him pity, only support. I shouldn't say this, and I will swear you to secrecy if I tell you." I hesitated to wait for an answer. None came, so I offered. "Well, I'm waiting."

"Max, you can be so mysterious, of course, I will do whatever you say."

"John had a close call and has realized how important you are to him. That is unless he knows another girl named Adele, but I really don't think so. His self-esteem may be suffering if he feels he may not be able to fly again. What I am trying to tell you is, he needs your support and not only your support, he needs you. Adele, on the way back, I saw a different man than I knew in Vietnam. He loved you when we left France to go to Vietnam, now he needs you as well. I don't need a crystal ball to predict the future." I just stopped and waited.

"Max, thank you so much for what you have told me. I was completely a basket case until I talked to you. Do you mind if I love you too?"

"I'm sorry lady, but I do not intend to be second best. I will accept that John is the best, and I will step aside. I'll pick you up at seven."

"Thank you."

I was very curious as to why Adele did not mention Sarah. I guess she could only think about John at the time. It was just as well; I needed a little more time before I talked to Sarah. I went back to my room and resumed putting a few things away. It occurred to me that I should call my parents. Before I did, I would have to get permission as to what I could tell them.

I walked over to headquarters, which was only a few blocks away. I found the Colonel talking to the base commander and a couple of high-ranking officers, one was a General, so I sat down to wait. The door was open to the Commander's office, and I could hear a little of what was being said. They were speaking in French, which limited what I could understand. I had been around people speaking French long enough to understand some of what they were talking about. It was no doubt about Vietnam and our squadron. It was also apparent that they were not entirely pleased with the role we had played. At times, the conversation became rather heated, and I could see the Colonel was being blamed for something. I couldn't take it anymore. I walked over to the doorway and knocked. The General jerked his head around and said, "What do you want?" He was speaking in English since he saw my US Navy uniform.

I said. "General, I was with Colonel Ambert and a member of the unit he was commanding in Vietnam, I think I can provide some helpful information."

The General just stared at me and said, "Commander, this is a French affair and to be very frank, none of your business."

"I would differ with that statement, General. I was assigned to the Legion by my country to help the Legion in a very difficult situation."

The General interrupted. "You were only an observer; how can that help with the fighting and decision making that our Commanders were faced with?"

"I can only give you one word, Sir, and that is experience. If I may, I would like to elaborate on that more to see if I would meet your qualifications for experienced."

The General seemed to calm down a bit and said. "Go on."

"I was in Korea and flew numerous missions off an aircraft carrier. I was in many battles and shot down twice. I spent almost a year in a Korean prison. I carried a load of experience to the Legion. That is one of the reasons my country asked me to help you, and you accepted. I was not eager to enter battle again, but I knew you were fighting a just cause, and I knew I could help. I'm not a mercenary, I have no desire to die in battle or to be maimed for the rest of my life. The beatings I took in a Korean prison camp have already had an adverse effect on me. I wanted to fly again, but not in combat. I went with the Legion to Vietnam as someone who could organize and help direct their operations in a combat zone. We entered your war at a time when you had already lost, and that was impossible to reverse. The decisions that caused that situation had already been made, perhaps even by some here in this room." I hesitated to see if I may have ruffled some feathers.

I continued. "You questioned my qualifications, and ability, to help with the operations of a fighting unit. General, I have been there, and I have done just that. I have fought alongside some of the finest fighting men in the world, men who would give their lives to help you as you would them." I hesitated and looked down at the floor.

I looked up and advanced toward the General, raising my voice slightly. "I, sir, had the privilege of doing that again. I flew with the equal of the men I had flown with in the US Navy, only these men were in the French Legion. That's right, General, I flew alongside these men of the French Legion in combat, and I have never seen braver or better-qualified men anywhere.

When the Commanding Officer of our squadron, John Roubalay, had his plane badly damaged, and it was apparent he could not make it back to our base, I went to help him. I knew that Colonel Ambert did not want me to go, but I went anyway. The commanding officer, John Roubalay, did go down and crashed in a field. In aiding him, I too was shot down. We spend three days on the ground before being picked up, and when we were, the chopper was attacked by Viet Minh. The commanding officer, John Roubalay, received three bullet wounds as we tried to get to the chopper. After he was down, not thinking of himself, he told me to save myself and get on the chopper. I refused to do this and helped him. He demonstrated courage and bravery as much as any man I have ever served in combat with."

I again hesitated and walked over to the Colonel, put my hand on his shoulder, and said. "I was with this man when he made the decisions that had to be made. Decisions that often had to be balanced with life and death on one end of the scale. It's easy, as we say in America, to be a Sunday morning quarterback and make the calls after they have happened the night before. That could be happening here. I never saw him make a bad call; I would have called them the same way myself. I am honored to have served the Legion under his command.

The General walked over to where I was standing and offered his hand to shake. "Thank you, Commander, I think you are right in what you said. Decisions on a battlefield are made under different circumstances than those made later by someone sitting behind a desk.

I think we have things under control here and I am sure it will work out well for everyone. I would like to offer my thanks, and I know the thanks of the Legion, for what you did." I thanked the General, turned, and shook the Colonel's hand and departed.

I still wanted to call my parents, but I was not sure what I could tell them. As I was pondering all this, the Colonel and base commander came out of the room followed by the General and his staff. I wasn't sure if it was appropriate, but I approached the General and asked him if it would be alright to tell my parents where I was and what I had been doing. The General appeared to ponder that question for a short time and said to go ahead and tell my family, but not to elaborate any more than was necessary. I thanked him and went to find a phone I could use for overseas calls.

As the call was going through, I tried to figure out what time it would be at home. It was too late to hang up, so I just let it go through. After about four rings, my mother answered the phone with a simple hello. "Hello, Mom, this is Max. I forgot about the time difference between here and home, hope it didn't startle you."

Mom's voice became very excited. "We have been worried sick about you, are you alright?"

"I'm fine, Mom. How are all of you?

"We are all doing well here. Where are you?"

"I'm in France and hope to be coming home soon."

"Where in the world have you been. We heard from you, but you never told us where you were. Have you been in France all this time?"

"No, Mom, I was helping France in another country where they were having some trouble."

"What kind of trouble?"

"They were fighting another country over a dispute. I went as an advisor."

"Thank goodness, I thought you may be in some fighting. We were worried sick."

"I did do some fighting, but it is all over now. I'm back in France and will be coming home soon."

"Can I stop worrying now?"

"Yes, Mom, you can stop worrying now."

The conversation continued. Dad wanted to talk, so I visited with him for a while. Dad does not like to talk on the phone because he has some difficulty hearing, so I was turned back over to Mom. That concluded the conversation, so we both told each other we loved them and hung up.

I looked at my watch and saw it was time to go get Adele. John had given me his car keys and told me to take his car. Adele only lives about twenty minutes from our base, so it was not a long drive. I parked and walked up to where Adele lived. I thought it would be better to do this because she may want to talk about John for a while. I was right, she wanted to know everything and wanted to know it right now. I filled her in on most of what had happened. She appeared to accept what I said without too much questioning. Adele was very concerned that John may not be able to return to flying. She thought that it would be very hard for him to accept.

"I wished I could tell you how to deal with John's ability to fly if that does happen, but I can't. I know he will need all your support, and I know that you will know how to deal with it. I think the Legion is a little more lenient than the US Navy would be, so flying may not be a problem at all."

Adele looked straight into my eyes with a very stern look and said, "Max, don't ever tell John I said this, but I wished John would give up flying."

"I know what you are saying, Adele, and you are right if you are thinking about the dangers of flying. It is dangerous. I can't really explain why a pilot feels the way he does, but I know it gets in your blood and won't let go. We know it is dangerous, but we won't let ourselves believe that.

A pilot thinks it's always the other guy that gets killed. Perhaps you have convinced yourself that it can't happen to you. That is the way it must be, Adele, if you ever let yourself be afraid it will diminish your chance to stay alive. A pilot must believe he can deal with anything. I can't

174

remember ever being afraid in an airplane. You may be concerned about something that could happen, but you can never express fear. If you do, I don't think you will live very long. Fear will make a pilot make mistakes, and there is absolutely no room for mistakes. They are all too often fatal. Adele, I am telling you this, so you know how John feels about flying. Not only John but every good pilot. I can't tell you how to deal with it, only what you will be dealing with."

"Thanks, Max, I appreciate your telling me all this. By the way, have you talked to Sarah yet?"

"No, I haven't. I'm not sure how to deal with Sarah. I know you are a very close friend of Sarah's. May I confide in you with something that will stay just between you and me?"

"You know you can, Max."

"I like Sarah, and I think she is a wonderful girl. The problem is not with Sarah, but with her fame. I don't need to tell you how a famous person such as Sarah can keep looking for a new adventure, and that adventure is in the form of the opposite sex. Sarah has already been married twice, and she is not that old. She already has a track record that scares me."

"I know what you are saying, Max. I wish I could tell you with certainty that it wouldn't happen again, but I can't. I think if Sarah found the right man, she would be completely different. I know you are different than anyone I have ever seen her date. If it could be anyone, it would be you. I am absolutely sure of this. Sarah is a very close friend of mine, and I know what a good person she is. I think she is a different person than she was when she was married before. I do know she likes you a lot."

"I think she likes me too, but how long would that last.? I like Sarah a lot too, but I'm afraid of her. I know I can't compete with her on the amount of money she makes. I might be out of a job if the Navy won't allow me to fly anymore. I guess it wouldn't work anyway if I was in the Navy. That brings up another fact that I would be completely dependent on her for everything. I certainly don't like that.

"Max, I wished I could give you the right advice. I think Sarah would love you enough for it to work, but I can't say for certain. Please don't just walk away, at least talk to Sarah. I know John, and I would welcome you as a permanent friend."

"Thanks, Adele, You and John are two of my favorite people. We will always be friends, no matter what happens. I think we better get going, John may be getting suspicious."

I drove Adele back to the base and delivered her to John. I told them to give me a call when Adele wanted to go home. I told them I would be in my room. I had a lot to think about.

CHAPTER XIII

I had so much to think about. So much had changed. I wasn't sure what would happen next. I knew I wasn't ready for whatever it was. I was sure now that I had lost Danny. I was convinced that Sarah would be a gamble, one that I was not sure I wanted to take. I did not think that the Navy would allow me to fly. I felt like I had lost everything I wanted or thought I would want. I had nowhere to go, nothing to turn to.

There was nothing on the horizon to give me hope. I sat there for a while feeling sorry for myself until I realized I was alive, and that meant a lot after all I had been through. I never was a quitter, and I am not about to quit now. If I don't have a path to follow, I will make a path. It was the best pep talk I had ever had, and I gave it to myself.

I knew I had to confront Sarah at some point. I knew it wouldn't be easy because I had started to like her, but I knew it had to happen, and I knew I could not let my feelings for her make me disguise what I knew was real. I decided to call her and ask her to accompany me on a date. This was as good a time as any and I had my courage up, so I decided to call. I dialed the phone hesitating on each number with uncertainty.

The phone was ringing as I nervously waited. Someone picked up the phone, and I heard the voice of an angel say hello in French. I wanted to slam the phone down and run for my life, but I couldn't move. I heard the same hello again. I just said, "Sarah."

There was an immediate response, "Max, is that you?"

"Yes, Sarah, it's me, Max."

"I am so happy you called. I knew you were back. I was worried you wouldn't call me. I was afraid you didn't want to see me again."

"That is why I am calling, I was wondering if you would care to have dinner with me soon, like maybe tomorrow night."

"I would love to have dinner with you then, but what about tonight? It's still early, and I am desperate to see you. It's been so long."

"Sarah, I don't think you knew that John was wounded. He is in the hospital here on the base. I picked up Adele a little earlier, so she could see him and spend a little time with him. I will have to take her back later."

"Is John badly injured?"

"It is not life-threatening, but it will take time to heal. John was hit in his right shoulder and right leg."

"Max, let me come out to see you and John, I can take Adele home later. I really want to see you, please."

"I would like to see you too, Sarah, just come right to the hospital and ask for John. I will go back over to the hospital and wait for you there."

I hurried back over to the hospital. I wanted to make sure it was alright with John and Adele to let Sarah come over. They were both agreeable, John said he would like to see her again since it had been a long time.

After Sarah arrived, we had a very nice visit. John was feeling better and looking better. It was good to have us all together again. I didn't get to spend any one on one time with Sarah. It was just the four of us, so we said goodnight knowing we would have dinner tomorrow evening.

The next morning, I went to the Colonel's office and asked if it would be alright if I made arrangements to return home. He told me that I was to receive a medal from the Legion. He wanted to have it photographed when it was pinned on me. They would release a story to my hometown paper as well as to other major newspapers. He wanted me to let myself be interviewed for that release.

He had talked to the US Navy. They would reimburse me for civilian travel when the Legion was through with me. I basically had permission to stay if the Legion needed me. I was then to return to the base I had left from, which was Alameda, California. This was Tuesday. The medal ceremony, which included John, the Colonel, and several of the other pilots as well as me, was scheduled for Saturday. I could leave on the following Monday. I did make a reservation to leave at that time.

I had a date with Sarah that evening. We planned to have dinner at the same quaint place we had dined at before. I was looking forward to seeing her. When she picked me up, I marveled at her beauty and knew why she was a movie star. We had a wonderful evening filled with laughter and tears that Sarah shed because I would be leaving. We returned to her house, just wanting to be close to each other. Sarah had a banquet to attend, related to a movie she had made, that she would attend on Friday night. She asked me if I would be her escort. I told her I might feel a little out of place not being able to converse in French. She assured me that she would be my interpreter and never leave my side. How could I refuse?

She asked me to stay at her home when I did not have to be on the base. She put it this way. "If you don't consider having me with you all the time, I will treat you so nice you will beg to stay and never want to leave. Then I will hold you captive for the rest of your life. I will never let you go and make you love me as much as I love you."

"Are you trying to tell me you want to take me prisoner? That would be considered being a captive. You know I was once a captive in Korea, I know all about it. You're not about to trick me into something like that. I'm wise to your kind."

We shared a make-believe dream that both of us knew could not happen without major changes in our lives. There were too many barriers, too many differences. I was sure it would be difficult at best to make it last. We spent most of our time together.

The banquet was an elaborate affair with all the important people in the French movie industries. Sarah was stunning when she went up to accept her award. I realized then it was not my world, but a make-believe world. Far too complicated for me and not what I wanted. It was apparent to me that a make-believe world would induce a make-believe life. Everything seemed to be artificial or fake. I could love Sarah, but it would have to be in a different world, a world I knew, and one Sarah had forgotten.

We spent a lot of time with John and Adele. John had proposed to Adele. They would set a wedding date for several months in the future. They asked me, and I agreed to be the best man. I promised to return to fulfill that promise.

The medal awards ceremony went well with lots of high-ranking Legion officers present. Of course, the politicians were all present too. John and I received the same medal, which was for bravery in combat. I also received a letter of thanks from the French government.

The day came for me to leave. It was a tearful event for both the girls. John and I shared a more solemn parting. Sarah and I made promises we knew could not be kept. I boarded the plane and watched France fade into the distance, becoming only a memory.

When I arrived in Alameda, I check in, tried to settle in, and get organized. The next day I was greeted by many of the pilots I had flown with in Korea. There had been a huge story with pictures when I had received my medal from the French Foreign Legion. I had numerous letters, including from my parents, and one from Danny. The one from my parents had nothing but praise. I anxiously opened the one from Danny. She said she was still seeing her boyfriend, but less frequent. She hoped we could always be friends and asked if I was still seeing the movie star. It was a rather short letter.

I reported into the Admiral's office, receiving a warm reception from all including the Admiral. We discussed at length what had happened in Vietnam and where the mistakes were made. The Admiral told me that he was certain the United States would get involved. He also said I would be valuable in supplying information on Vietnam, and my opinion on the mistakes made by the French.

I asked him if I would be considered for flying again. He did not know but promised to get me in to be examined. It would be entirely up to the doctors, and there was nothing he could do once they made their decision. I told him that it did not interfere with my flying for the French Foreign Legion. That the restricted movement of my left shoulder was not great, and not noticeable because my left arm was used mostly for things like the throttle that did not require a lot of dexterity. He again expressed his thanks for a job well done, and that he was going to recommend a decoration for me also. I thanked him and left.

I was required to have a complete physical as soon as possible, which was scheduled in two days. In the meantime, I requested leave to go home and spend some time with my parents. I had talked to them on the phone. They said I was a hero in Cedar Rapids, Iowa. They also said they had been contacted by the Mayor. He said the city was planning a reception of sorts with a recognition for my participation in Korea and Vietnam.

I wrote to my parents telling them to ask the city not to do anything. If they did, it should be for all who served in the war. I would gladly be a part of such a celebration as long as the others would be included.

I took my physical and was told the results would have to be sent in to be evaluated by a board. This could take several weeks. I would be notified when they published the results.

I requested leave and was granted thirty days. I would leave in three days. I wrote to my parents and told them.

CHAPTER XIV

The flight home was filled with wondering about my friends that I had not seen for a long time, how my parents would react when they knew where I had been and what I had done. I thought about Danny and Sarah. My parents told me there was a lot said about me in the release from the French. The pictures that had reached them when I escorted Sarah to the banquet also was newsy. They said that some folks thought of me as a celebrity, which I did not like nor want.

When I did arrive at the airport in Cedar Rapids, I was greeted by the mayor with a letter of appreciation for my service. There was a brief interview with the newspaper. I was very adamant about the fact that I was only one of many and that all the people who served deserved this recognition. I would only accept it under those conditions. I would accept it for all who served. I think my Mom, Dad, and Sister were pleased with what I had said.

I was asked to speak at an assembly in one of the school's auditoriums. It was designed to inform people what had taken place in Vietnam, and the reason France had been involved. I did agree to that since I thought all people should be aware of that situation. All people should know that the suppression of people's rights does occur. That all nations must stand together to fight this suppression, and let all people live in freedom and as they choose.

I think it turned out well. I had enough first-hand knowledge to portray it as it is in reality. Not to sugar coat it, but to let people know that this does happen, and there are nations that will fight to protect weaker nations right to live as they choose.

After the presentation, I took the time to renew some old friendships. It had been several years since I had seen many of them. So much had changed, and so many of my friends had changed. Most were married with children.

I was asked several times why I wasn't married, mostly why I didn't get together with the French movie star. I just told them I didn't have time; I was too busy fighting a war.

My college sweetheart was there with her husband. She still looked radiant and lovely. I tried to figure out what went wrong with that relationship. It didn't take long to remember that she did not want me to join the Navy and issued me an ultimatum. It was simply, her or the Navy. I am not sure I made the right choice, but I think it was the better choice for me.

For some reason, Danny kept creeping back into my thoughts. I wished so much that could have had a different ending. I wondered if I did the right thing. She was only dating this guy. I should have fought for what I wanted. I was a fool and acted like some juvenile. I wondered if it was too late. I treated her so badly that I am sure she would not have anything to do with me now. After all, what girl would want to put up with someone acting the way I did?

I had known her for such a short time; and not sure we really knew each other. If I could get up enough courage, I would try to write to her or call her. Perhaps writing would be better, she may hang up on me.

My mental argument ended when my parents came over to see if I was ready to go home. I told my Mom that I had made the biggest mistake of my life and didn't know how or if I could correct it.

Mom asked me to tell her more. I told her what I had been thinking about.

"Max, I tried to tell you that, but you wouldn't listen. We can talk about that at home."

On the ride home, we talked about my presentation. We all thought it went well. It was decided that I had given the people a look at the real world. One that most don't stop to think about.

When we arrived home, Dad and I decided to have a beer. We sat down at the kitchen table and started to visit. Mom came in, poured herself a little glass of wine, and asked if she could join us.

The look on her face was telling me that I was about to endure some of her wrath. Not a bad wrath, but a sort of good wrath. I am not sure there is such a thing as good wrath. However, I knew I was about to have a severe reprimand coming my way.

Mom began, "Max, you have acted like a spoiled three-year-old. You treated Danny horribly. I don't know if or even why she would want anything to do with you. She threw you an olive branch, and you stepped on it. "Dad slid his chair back from the table as if to get out of the line of fire. Mom continued, "Danny had every right to date someone else. She thought you were not even alive. She could have gone and sat at your grave till resurrection day. Is that what you wanted?"

"No, Mom."

"Danny and I have talked on the phone many times and have become good friends. She stopped seeing the man she was seeing, but you wouldn't know this because she made me promise not to tell you. However, I am now because you need to know. Danny thinks you are involved with that French movie star and don't have feelings for her. I am not sure about the first, but I am beginning to believe the other."

Mom shoved a piece of paper over to me and said, "Here is Danny's phone number, go call her right now and at least apologize to her. She does deserve at least that."

"I'm not sure I can, Mom."

"Max, Danny deserves at least an apology. You can surely do that."

"I know you are right Mom; you have always given me good advice. I think she will slam the phone down, but I will do as you say. Must I do it now?"

Mom seemed to think awhile. "No, Max, but I think it would be a good idea. If you put it off, it will only be more difficult."

I looked at Dad. He was giving me that old, "you're on your own" look.

I retrieved the number, and reluctantly started for the living room phone. I was not sure what I would or should say. I hesitated on each number I dialed. I listened to it ring six times. There was not an answer. I was almost relieved to be able to hang it up.

"I'll try later, Mom."

We retreated to the kitchen. I opened another beer and could see I was shaking. I think Mom saw it too.

"Are you alright, Max?"

"Yeah, I am. It's just that I am afraid Danny will hang up on me and not give me a chance to try to explain what an idiot I have been."

The phone rang. Since Mom was the closest, she picked it up and said hello. The rest that I heard was in broken sentences. "No, it wasn't me. No, you're not bothering me. How did your day go?" This continued for several minutes. Finally, Mom handed the phone to me and said, "I think you may want to talk to this person."

I took the phone from my mother and offered a hello. "Hello, Max, this is Danny. If you want to hang up, you can." It was as though someone had struck a blow to my chest.

"I don't want to hang up. I want to ask you to forgive me. I know I did everything wrong, but I thought you did not want me in your life. I thought you had found someone that you wanted to be with. It was never that, Danny."

"Max, I was hurt that you wouldn't even allow me to contact you. It was a shock when I heard your voice on the phone when you first called. I was confused and not sure of what I was saying. Couldn't you understand that?"

"I can now, Danny. I guess I was also shocked and didn't know how to react. I hope you will understand that also."

"I do, Max. I guess we both made a mistake, but that is over, and you are involved with a movie star now."

"I am not involved with her or any other girl. You're the reason I am not. The thoughts of you allowed me to survive my imprisonment in Korea. They kept me going through all the tough times, but they also devastated me after I thought I had lost you.

I never stopped loving you, Danny. I know I never could. We only knew each other for a short time, but I have never been surer of anything in my entire life. Can you forgive me? I am begging for another chance; will you give me that? I will get down on my knees and beg right now if I must. I can't live without you, Danny."

I could hear a sniffling on the phone. I knew Danny was starting to cry. She had a habit of that. I secretly hoped they were happy tears. "Danny, I hear that you are crying, I hope that is a positive answer."

There was a pause and another sniffle. I only heard a weak, "Yes," followed by more sniffles.

"I want to see you as soon as I can. Will you allow me to come to wherever you are?"

Danny had regained her composure and answered. "Max, I want to meet your Mom and Dad, can I come there? I can get on the next plane if you let me."

"I'm not sure that is soon enough, but it will have to do. Let me know when you have your flight. I love you, Danny."

"I love you too, Max. Goodbye for now."

"Goodbye."

Danny was on a plane the next day, arriving at about noon. I was waiting at the gate when she arrived. When she saw me, she dropped the bag she was carrying and ran to me, falling into my arms. I didn't think I could ever let go of her, but I did.

Danny left the Army. I stayed in the Navy but never flew again.

The only thing left to say is, "They lived happily ever after."

Made in the USA
Middletown, DE
15 August 2019